Captured
by a Spy

To our dear Zachariah
whose name means
God Remembers

Ben and Zack Series, Book 1

Captured by a Spy

L. Travis

Baker Books
A Division of Baker Book House Co
Grand Rapids, Michigan 49516

© 1995 by L. Travis

Published by Baker Books
a division of Baker Book House Company
P.O. Box 6287 Grand Rapids, MI 49516-6287

Printed in the United States of America

Library of Congress Cataloging-in-Publication Data
Travis, L., 1931–
    Captured by a spy / L. Travis.
        p. cm.—(Ben and Zack series ; bk. 1)
    Summary: Two boys, one black and the other white, are kid-
napped from their Tarrytown, N.Y., home by Confederate spies
and taken north along the Hudson River and into Canada.
    ISBN: 0-8010-8915-8
    1. United States—History—Civil War, 1861–1865—Juvenile
fiction. [1. Adventure and adventurers—Fiction. 2. United
States—History—Civil War, 1861–1865—Fiction. 3. Tarrytown
(N.Y.)—Fiction. Lucille, 1931–   Ben and Zack series ; bk. 1.
PZ7.T68915Cap   1995
[Fic]—dc20   94-27059

Contents

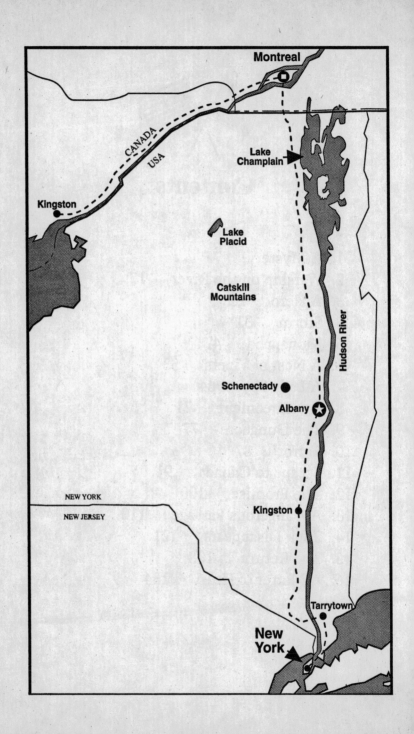

1

A Mystery

The baker's shop was empty except for Ben. As she handed him his change, the shopkeeper leaned across the counter. Her voice was low. "I tell you, young master, New York City is no place to be these days. There's them as is stirring up common folks. Mark my words, there's trouble brewing."

"Yes, ma'am. Soon as the coach is ready my father and I will be going back home to Tarrytown," Ben answered.

The bell on the shop door rang, and a woman entered. As the shopkeeper turned to her new customer, Ben made his escape into the street. He had heard the rumors of unrest in the city, but at least here it looked quiet enough. Large warehouses and office buildings ringed the square. Heavily loaded carts mingled with the fine carriages of shoppers and businessmen. Above it all a thick smoky haze hung unmoving in the July heat.

His father was still in the ticket office. Ben leaned lazily against one giant wheel of the empty coach as he spun the shiny new half-dollar the shopkeeper had given him in change. Before he could catch it the coin seemed to spring from his palm onto the cobblestones where it rolled halfway across the square and beneath a black carriage with red and silver trim.

The horse and carriage faced away from Ben so that he could not see its occupants. The coin had stuck between two cobblestones midway under the carriage. On his knees he crawled between the back wheels to reach for it. At that moment the horse, disturbed by a passing cart, jerked left, and the shifting wheel caught the edge of Ben's jacket beneath it.

He tried to pull the coattail from under the heavy wheel, but it stuck fast. As he worked frantically to loosen it, he heard voices coming from the carriage overhead.

"The risk is great, but my men are ready to deliver the goods." The voice sounded like that of an elderly man. Ben couldn't help listening.

"You are a trusted friend of my father's." The second voice belonged to a younger person. "Without your help the South would be poorer." Startled, Ben listened closely. The South meant one thing. No Northerner would talk about helping the South now that they were at war with each other. Yet someone right here in the North was talking about helping the enemy.

"I wish that you would let another take your place," the older voice said. "This is far too dangerous a mission for you."

"Don't fear, old friend. My father would have

come himself if his health permitted, but I am well disguised. Besides, these days it is not wise to place such a large amount of money as this in too many hands."

"Well, if you must do this yourself, then God be with you. The least I can do for your father is exchange Confederate money for Union until such time as this war is over. He is not only an old friend, but one of our best suppliers of fine cotton. All of us suffer now that trade between us is outlawed."

"I am grateful for all you've done, sir," the young voice said. "The contact your man has arranged with the gentleman called the General will be most helpful to us. His is a clever plan to bring supplies from Canada down the Hudson River to New York City. While the Yankees are hunting down our ships on the high seas he is bringing in supplies and medicines right under their noses."

"I daresay, you will need every coin in that bag," the older voice added. "The General and his men do not come cheap. Now, you have the password, and you know the location where you will be picked up?"

Ben did not hear the answer. He worked furiously at his coattail. Whoever was inside the carriage might decide to move at any moment. Ben did not see the driver of the carriage returning with a package for his employer until the man's large hand gripped his shoulder from behind.

"Just what do you think you're doing under there, lad?" the big man growled.

"Nothing, sir. My change rolled under, and when I tried to get it the horse moved the carriage. My coat is stuck under the wheel," Ben said, his heart beating loudly.

With a mighty push the man moved the wheel enough to release Ben's coat. "Now you get out of here, and don't let me catch you doing such a fool thing again. Do you hear?" he said.

"Yes, sir. I won't, thank you, sir." Ben clutched the coin he had snatched from between the cobblestones. Across the square his father was just leaving the ticket office. He motioned for Ben to hurry. The coach was ready, and most of the passengers had boarded. Ben found a seat across from his father. The last passenger to arrive was a young man carrying a black satchel. Ben made room for him between himself and the window.

For the next few minutes Ben's mind whirled with the mysterious conversation he had overheard. He wished he had seen who was inside the carriage. Should he have told someone? But what proof did he have? If someone was using the river to smuggle supplies from Canada to help the South, that meant whoever was doing it would pass right by Tarrytown. The coach swayed as the horse's iron-shod hoofs rang sharply. They were getting farther and farther away from the square and the mystery carriage. Then, without warning, Ben landed violently against the stout gentleman seated across from him as the coach came to a sudden stop.

Ben sat back on his seat and mumbled, "Sorry,

sir," then bent to help his father pick up the gentleman's scattered packages. Wondering what had stopped the coach, he pulled the last parcel from under the seat and handed it to its owner. As he sat back, the young gentleman seated next to him made room for him at the coach window.

In the street a wall of old furniture, barrels, and bricks barred the way. From a shop behind the barricade, four men stepped toward the coach. One of them wore a baker's apron and waved a long-barreled rifle. He pointed the gun to the north as he spoke. "The road ahead is closed. You best be going back to Murray Hill and north from there to the post road."

Ben felt his father's hand on his shoulder. Leaning above Ben, he shouted from the window, "Can you give us any news, sir? Are the rumors true, then, of rioting in the city?"

"The word is a mob has set fire to the government's draft office down on Third Avenue and Forty-Sixth Street, sir. Another crowd is burning down the Negroes' shanties." The man waved his gun toward the streets beyond the barricade. "The police can't hold out much longer up there. 'Tis not safe on the streets, you'd best take warning, sir. Every cutthroat gang in the city has joined the fighting."

Ben's father shook his head. "I was afraid it would come to that."

The stout man said loudly, "We have nothing to do with rioters. We're gentlemen here." Ben saw him take a pinch of powdery snuff from a small snuffbox, inhale it, and sneeze.

Again the baker warned them. "Nobody's asking questions today, sir. There be a gentleman run into a mob down by the waterfront. Mistook he was for a government man, dead before it were noticed that he weren't. You best be off quick, while the road's still open."

With an oath, the driver turned the horses in the direction of Murray Hill. Ben steadied his feet against the floor. This visit to the city was fast changing into something more than an ordinary trip.

The horses were galloping, but at one street Ben caught a fleeting glimpse of a black man running from a crowd. Behind him some white men shouted and shook their fists as they ran after him. A smell of burning carried on the air. Ben could not see the fire, but in the distance dark clouds of smoke rose in the sky. Gradually the smells and sounds of the riots faded as they sped on.

Next to Ben, the young man, who had not spoken a word since coming aboard the coach, leaned his head back and pulled his hat down over his eyes. Ben studied his smooth, narrow face and guessed the man was not many years older than he. How could the fellow sleep? It was hot and, wiping sweat from his face with the back of his sleeve, Ben looked questioningly at his father. He didn't dare tell him about the conversation he had overheard, at least not here in the crowded coach. Instead he asked, "Do you reckon there will be more trouble, Pa?"

"I doubt we've seen the last of it yet," his father replied. "We've fought three wars, all with volunteer soldiers. This war over slavery is different. When a man's hard put to feed his own children he may be against slavery in his heart but feel the war to free slaves down south is no concern of his." He paused to shift his long legs in the cramped space. "Under the new law if a man's name is on what's called the draft lists he must join the army or pay three hundred dollars to buy his way out. The rich can pay and stay home, but the poor have no choice but to go. The rioters want to overturn a law they think is unfair."

"Pardon," the stout gentleman interrupted. "I believe there are also businessmen in the city who have no love for this war, since their cotton trade with the South is cut off."

"Yes, it's true," Ben's father agreed. "Many have lost much. But this war against slavery must go on until it is won."

"Reverend, you'll permit me to correct you," the man said. "Surely our northern troops do not fight to free slaves but to save the United States from being cut in two. We cannot allow the South to become a separate nation." He cleared his throat and went on. "As for these city mobs rioting against proper government, they should be whipped. They're ignorant, lazy, without loyalty to anything but their bellies."

Ben's father leaned his tall, broad body back against the coach seat. His clean-shaven face was unsmiling as his steel-blue eyes searched the stout man's face. "Sir," he said, "until the sickness of slavery is abolished this country will never be whole. And I think, sir, we are all somewhat loyal to our bellies in one way or another."

As Ben tried to hide a grin, the sound of distant gunshots startled him. He would have plenty to tell Zack when they got back home. His friend's dark face and tightly curled black hair flashed before Ben's mind. Some folks in Tarrytown might look down on the Negroes, but they would never burn down the Negroes' houses the way the rioters were doing in the city. Even the Sorley boys, who gave Ben and Zack trouble because Zack was a Negro, did not go around burning folks out.

He had known Zack as far back as he could remember. Zack and his granny lived in a small house on the edge of the woods behind the parsonage where Ben lived. He knew his father would take Zack's side as quickly as he would Ben's if Zack was in the right. Granny, with her shining dark face and cloudy old eyes, treated both boys like her own.

Hours later the coachman pulled the horses to a stop in front of the Tarrytown Inn. Ben followed the other passengers from the coach. As he glanced toward the Hudson River lapping against the town dock, he thought again of the strange conversation he had overheard. Who was smuggling supplies, and what kind of boat were they using? All kinds of small boats, steamboats, and barges passed along the river. He ought to have said something in New York City. Was it too late now? The nagging thought kept coming to him that he had no proof. The only thing he had to go on was the sound of two strangers' voices.

His father strode ahead, and Ben hurried to catch up. On the hilltop that overlooked the town the parsonage's white paint gleamed in the sun. From the corner of his eye Ben saw Widow Bell's large black cat raise one paw toward a passing butterfly. Too lazy to give chase, the cat settled back into a patch of mint. After New York City, sleepy old Tarrytown seemed like a place where nothing ever happened. But what if people who sympathized with the South were smuggling supplies for the South right past Tarrytown?

Ben might have said something if his father had not gone straight to visit a sick church member and his mother to choir practice.

Asleep in his room, Ben did not hear the sound of riders gallop into town shortly after midnight. The men, dressed in army uniforms, pulled to a stop in front of the office of the provost marshal, head of the military police. The marshal stood waiting. One of the soldiers handed down a saddlebag. He spoke for a few minutes then motioned his men to follow and headed back out of town.

The marshal slipped inside his office. A few minutes later he reappeared without the saddlebag and locked the door behind him. The secret transfer of

16

New York City's draft lists with all the names of men to be called into the army had gone smoothly. The marshal yawned and headed for home.

In the shadows behind the tavern two figures watched the marshal leave. "You must get word to our people in the city, John," one whispered.

"Aye, that I will, young sir," the other said.

2

Warship on the River

Tarrytown was preparing for battle! Cheers rose from the townsfolk gathered at the dock. On the hill where they watched, Ben and Zack could see the smoke pouring into the blue sky as the government warship *Eagle* steamed up the Hudson River. Someone had uncovered the secret transfer of New York City's draft lists to the marshal's office, and a mob from the city was forming to come and burn the lists. All of Tarrytown had turned out to see the warship sent by the government to help guard the lists.

On deck the ship carried the biggest guns the boys had ever seen this close. "You reckon they'll fire on the mob if it comes?" Zack asked.

"Guess she will fire if she has to. Mostly she's here to warn off the rioters, Pa says," Ben answered.

An old navy man, standing next to Ben, lifted his cane in the direction of the ship. "Way she's sitting out there midriver, she'd take out the whole waterfront." He looked down at the boys. "Don't think she'll be firing. Leastwise this town'll be a sorry sight if she does." The old sailor pointed with his cane behind them up where the main road into town came through. "Won't even see any mob 'til they're right in town. Better be clearing out of here before any fireworks, boys. That ship'll blow anything standing in the way to pieces."

Zack's face looked grim. "I best be goin' down to the store."

Ben nodded. "I'll come with you." He knew what Zack was thinking. Zack's Uncle Uriah's small candy store stood right in the line of the ship's cannon fire. Until now it had not occurred to Ben that the town might be in real danger.

By the time the boys pushed through to the little store that was squeezed between two larger buildings, Uncle Uriah was locking the door. At his feet lay sacks and bundles.

"Where you been, Zack? Don't you hear the marshal sayin' colored folks got to clear out to Buttermilk Hill till it's safe to come down?" he scolded. "You done hear 'bout New York City. Them folks don't want to fight no war, so they's fightin' with the gov'ment 'bout gettin' drafted. They be comin' here to make trouble." He bent over the bundles to check a sack. "They be blamin' colored folks, burnin' down poor folks' shanties. The marshal don't want nothin' like that here."

Zack took the bundles Uriah handed him and slung one over his shoulder, the other under his arm. "You sure you hear the marshal right?" he asked.

"Look up there, son. You see that?" Uriah pointed in the direction of Buttermilk Hill. Families of

Negroes carrying bundles of all shapes were heading toward the hill.

"But you don't have to go, Uriah," Ben said.
"Zack can stay with me, and I know my ma will
put you and Granny up, too."

Uriah looked at Ben and shook his head. His
voice was gentle. "Granny already gone up with
the young ones. She be waitin' for Zack and me."
He bent to pick up another sack and lifted it onto
his back. "Your ma and pa be mighty good folks.
Don't want no trouble comin' down on them.
Plenty work to do gettin' folks settled on the hill.
You come on now, Zack." He handed Zack his
ancient hunting rifle, and with the last small bun-
dle under his arm began the long walk to the hill.

"Reckon I gotta go," Zack said. "You take care,
Ben, you hear? If you be needin' me, you know
where I'm at."

A lump rose in Ben's throat. "Guess you'll be
helping Uriah and your granny for a spell. Soon as
there's any news, I'll come," he promised. "Reckon
you'll hear the guns if they do use them."

Zack smiled broadly. "That be for sure," he said.

One of the marshal's men, a lanky fellow who
had been barking orders to the men assigned to him,
strode over to Ben and Zack. "Ain't you heard, boy,"
he shouted at Zack, "the marshal's order for your
kind to get out of town? Now get."

Angrily Ben turned to face the man, but before he
could speak a heavy hand gripped his shoulder. Ben
spun around to see his father. "Pa," he spluttered.

"The boy's name is Zackariah, and it means 'God remembers,'" his father said calmly.

Deliberately the man spat on the ground close to Ben and his father. "I got my orders," he muttered, turned his back, and walked away.

"Some folks have no manners at all," his father said and smiled. He placed his large hand firmly on Zack's shoulder. "You'll be needed up on the hill, Zack. I saw your granny a while back, and she'll be wanting your help setting up shelters. These are hard times we're living in, but the light of freedom is shining, and nothing is going to change that. Remember the meaning of your name, Zack."

Zack nodded. "I won't never forget, sir."

Ben lingered to watch Zack go toward Buttermilk Hill, while his father returned to Broadway. By the time Ben reached Broadway his father and a crowd of men were standing in front of the Tarrytown Inn listening to the marshal.

As Ben approached, the marshal, a short, stocky broad-shouldered man with a temper to match, said loudly, "The last thing we want is a warship firing on the town. But the draft lists are government property, and here they stay until the government moves them. Now, we'll need the help of every gun and every able-bodied man."

Ben heard his father's voice equally loud and insistent. "Surely we must use peaceful means first. Let me talk with their leaders, reason with them."

"You'll have your say, Reverend, but remember I warned you. If they come they won't be in the mood for a sermon. My men are posted along the road so we'll know in plenty of time soon as they're spotted. The word is they won't reach here before midday tomorrow. Meanwhile I suggest, gentlemen, that you go home and prepare."

Ben stared at the marshal's grim face. The idea of a battle in Tarrytown began to be all too real.

3

A Hero

Nothing stirred the heat that had settled in his room, and Ben tossed fitfully. He would rather have been up with Zack on Buttermilk Hill. Turning over to find a cool spot on the sheet he told himself he would be up at dawn. Bright sunlight streamed into his room by the time he opened his eyes. Why hadn't anyone called him? Halfway down the stairs he stopped, caught by the sharp tone of his mother's voice coming from behind the closed kitchen door.

"Why can't some of the Negroes come here, Stewart? We have room. Zack could stay with Ben. If necessary they could hide in the cellar. I thought of it all last night. Surely some of the other families are willing to help. Why should they be camped up there on the hill worrying that some crazy mob might hunt them down?"

Quietly Ben made his way to the closed door to hear better. His father's voice came through clear and firm. "You know the marshal is right, Sarah. If they stayed in town it might be the spark to set that mob off. They'll be safe enough on Buttermilk Hill.

By now they're settled out of sight. With that fool gunboat on the river we'd all be better off up there."

"I suppose you're right, but this is the North, Stewart. The law is supposed to protect them."

"That mob has one thing on its mind, Sarah: those draft lists. If we can convince them to go back home for their own good it will all be over. I'll be back, my love."

Ben came to life instantly. He was in the dining room by the time his father appeared. His mother brought in the serving bowl of porridge. His father stood in the doorway.

Ben saw the empty plate and bowl at his father's place. His father had already eaten. "I'm sorry, Pa. I must have overslept. I can be ready in no time."

For a moment his father stared at him. "I expect you to stay here with your mother, Ben," he said quietly.

"Pa, please let me come with you. I'm nearly twelve, and I can handle a gun. Please let me come."

His father's face was stern. "Would you take up a gun so lightly, son? Hunting game is one thing; raising a gun against a fellow human being is another. I do not want you downtown at all, and I mean that." Before Ben could say more he was gone. Ben clenched his jaw angrily.

"Ben," his mother said softly, "you know how your father feels about guns. He'd give his life to free the slaves, but there is no hatred in his heart for any man, North or South, not even for the men, whoever they are, in that mob."

She smoothed his hair back from his forehead, then tilted Ben's chin up to look in his eyes. "You're so like your father, same mop of brown hair, same stubborn chin. There's no finer man whose footsteps you could follow, son. He just doesn't want you where you might get hurt." Her eyes went to the dishes waiting to be done. "My granda always said, 'Best thing to clear a body's mind is a good solid hour of hoeing.'"

Ben never won an argument with the absent Granda. Working furiously he finished the last row of string beans and flung the weeds onto the refuse pile. He had to know what was going on. The marshal had said the mob could reach town by midmorning.

The tall beech tree on the hill stood like a ready-made watchtower. He and Zack had climbed it a hundred times. The tree was older than anybody could remember. Its huge dark-silver trunk lifted dozens of branches that angled and twisted to form snug perches. Ben climbed easily.

Perched on one of the highest limbs he could clearly see the center of town below. A crowd of men stood in front of the inn. The post road that led into town was empty. To the right the river stretched its widest, over two miles between Tarrytown and the cliffs on the far side.

Offshore the government warship waited. Ben's arm and shoulder, pressed tightly against the tree, began to ache, and he moved farther out on the limb. A week before, when he and Zack had matched their flexed muscles, Zack's were bigger.

"Ain't nothin'," Zack had said. "You still read better. But Mistress Capp say she'll be fixin' that soon, now I'm workin' for her." He laughed. "Everybody know she be the best teacher 'round here." It was true. Mistress Capp, retired from school teaching, needed help with her chores, but her tongue was still fine.

A knot tightened in Ben's stomach as he remembered reading yesterday's newspaper. His mother had cried over the report of the burning of a Negro orphanage, which forced the orphans to flee. "The poor lambs," she had said, "without a roof over their heads." A Negro man had been hung and others beaten. The governor had called for the militia to help police regain control of the city. Ben stared at the empty road below. What kind of mob was coming? Were these the same ones who had burned and looted in New York City? If anybody laid a hand on Zack he would have to take Ben too.

Not a speck of dust showed down the road. Hunger rumbled Ben's empty stomach. If he hurried he could grab something to eat and still be back in time.

The warm smell of gingerbread drew him to the kitchen. Ben helped himself to a handful of the cookies cooling on the table. His mother lifted a pot from the stove and set it aside to cool.

"That's almost the last of the molasses," she remarked.

"Ma," Ben said eagerly, "I could run into town to Bailey's. He might have gotten molasses in on Monday's boat. It won't take me long at all."

"Benjamin Stewart Able, you'll do no such thing." His mother stood with her hands on her hips, her mouth looking worried. "You know the town's shut up tight."

"But, Ma, what if Pa and the men can't stop them? What if Pa needs us?"

"Trouble comes running when it comes," she replied. Ben's mother was only a little taller than Ben. Her small face was plain and kind, her dark hair thick under the day cap she wore at home. Her gray eyes snapped now as she said, "Ben, it's been a long time since I've climbed a tree, though I once managed as good as any of my brothers. Do you reckon we could see much from that old beech out back?"

It was a wonder! Ben was sweating as they climbed. Looking back, he waited and gave advice. "Hold that limb. Pull up till your foot can rest on that one there." Ben swallowed hard as they climbed higher and higher till they reached the place where he and Zack usually sat.

"A body could get used to it again, I guess," his mother said, breathing hard.

Ben let out his breath in a whistle. This was the last place he'd expected to see his mother.

"Ben, they're coming." Her voice was almost a whisper.

Ben looked intently toward the post road. His

heart thumped loudly. A crowd of men were coming. Behind them were at least two wagons loaded with others. In front of the inn the townsmen stood waiting, all except a familiar tall figure in dark clothes who walked slowly toward the post road.

Ben watched as his father moved closer and closer to the mob. It seemed they would clash any moment. "Why doesn't he go back?" Ben cried. Horrified, he saw some in the mob raise their guns above their heads and wave them angrily. But his father had raised his arms too, the way he often did in church during a sermon. He was not holding a gun. The front line of the mob slowly halted.

Ben saw his father lower his arms and point to the river where the warship waited. Tense minutes passed. Ben's eyes were burning with the strain to see. Once more his father raised his arms. His face lifted toward the sky as if he were praying. When he finally lowered his arms he seemed to be talking with the crowd.

Slowly the mob began to break up into little groups. Some of them hesitated, then turned away from the town. The wagons were going, and others followed till it looked like they were all heading back the way they had come. Ben still tightly clutched the branch next to him. Were they really going back? Then suddenly men from the town were streaming toward his father.

Ben felt like he was just awakening from a dream. He looked at his mother and swallowed hard. With one hand she gripped the tree branch; with the other she covered her face and wept.

By the time they reached the bottom of the tree, Ben knew it had been dumb to let his mother climb it. Her hair had come loose, and her hitched-up skirts kept catching on branches. Just as they reached the last of the branches her foot twisted in a narrow Y. Limping and red faced she held Ben's shoulder all the way to the kitchen.

"Now, young man, I suppose you can't wait to be off. Well, go on, but not one word about this. I want no gossips telling how the preacher's wife caught her foot climbing a tree. Benjamin Stewart Able, promise me you won't tell a word of this to anyone."

"I promise, Ma. You sure you're okay?" Ben's hand was on the latch, his feet ready to run.

As he pushed through the crowd to his father, Ben heard the man who had called Zack a boy say, "Well now, Reverend, whatever you told that mob must have been mighty powerful. You preaching that sermon next Sunday, I just might come." Laughter broke out among the men who stood near him urging him on. "Guess maybe that warship out there helped some too." Turning away he called over his shoulder, "This calls for a celebration, boys."

A number of men followed him to the tavern. Ben heard one of them say loudly, "Ought to jail them all, the whole bunch of copperheads." Northerners who sided with the South were often called copperheads after a secret society of people who aided the South however they could and who wore lapel pins cut from copper. Copperhead was also the name of a poisonous snake.

The marshal grinned. He scratched his chin and said, "Reverend, if I hadn't seen it with my own eyes, I'd never have believed anything less than an order from one of their own leaders could have turned back that mob. Of course, we know you're a man of God."

Someone called out, "I say he's a hero."

As they walked home Ben felt a deep pride.

"I suppose you'll be wanting to run off to Buttermilk Hill?" his father said. There was a lightness in his voice as if a weight had left him.

"I sure was thinking on it," Ben replied hopefully.

"Go along, then. I'll let your mother know."

"Thanks, Pa." Ben walked quickly in the direction of Buttermilk. He was about to leave the road for the path through the woods when a wagon came rumbling from behind.

Jake Sorley pulled his horse to a slow amble alongside Ben. "Hear your pa's a hero. Some folks do say your pa didn't want any of them good copperheads killed. You reckon he knew some of them fellows? Or maybe some of them knew him. You think your pa was saving the town or them copperheads from getting blown up by the warship like they deserve?" Jake whipped up the horse and plunged the wagon past Ben as he yelled, "Yellowbelly snake copperheads ain't good for nothing but stomping on."

"You trying to say my pa is a copperhead?" Ben yelled back glaring at the retreating wagon. All the Sorley boys had mean ways, and Jake was the worst.

Maples and elms grew thick near the path. The cool shade of the woods felt good. Ben's mind was on Jake Sorley's words when a twig snapped. He looked up as Zack stepped from behind a tree.

4

Storm

While they walked Ben told Zack what had happened in town. When he finished Zack said, "Only one way to see that *Eagle* up close, Ben, 'fore she goes."

Ben nodded. "Guess we better raft out there tonight. By morning she'll be pulling up anchor and leaving." With low voices they made their plans.

The house was quiet. Ben waited to be sure his folks were asleep before he got out of bed and slipped into his clothes. His moccasins made no sound on the stairs. The heavy bolt on the kitchen door slid back without a sound.

The warm night air closed about Ben. Clouds hid the moon, and stars made the old beech tree look strange, less friendly in the dark. Every inch of the trail through the woods down to the river was familiar, but now the path was nowhere to be seen in the heavy darkness of the woods. Fumbling a bit, Ben lit the lantern he had brought. Its small glow was enough to show him the path a foot or so at a time. After a while he heard the river slapping against the bank. Between the river and the woods the railroad tracks lay long and black.

"Ben, that you?" came Zack's voice.

"That you, Zack?" Ben asked.

Zack had already uncovered their homemade raft. As he struggled to keep the lantern upright, Ben helped Zack carry the raft down to the river's edge.

"Careful, Ben, or she'll swamp," Zack said, his feet sliding on the muddy bank. Ben held tightly and strained to keep the raft steady as it dipped into the water. On board Zack held the raft pole against the river bottom until Ben slid on next to him. Ben placed the lantern next to Zack, then took the pole and pushed off. Swiftly the raft began to move out away from the black shoreline. A stiff breeze blew from behind them.

"It's a good thing the moon ain't shining now, or we'd be spotted quick as anything by the watch. Better blow out the lamp, Zack." Without the lantern's light, heavy darkness covered the boys. For a minute Ben saw nothing, then as his eyes adjusted he began to pick out shapes and bits of the river. In the distance a light showed where the warship lay at anchor.

"Sure is dark, Ben. Can't see where this old raft stop and the river begin," Zack said, shifting his weight.

"Watch it, Zack, or she'll tip. I can barely see my own feet. Better stay in close to shore until we get near her," he added.

Small waves rose and fell with the raft. Zack sat

back slowly. "Ben, we're really movin'. Feels like the wind's pickin' up some."

Ben lowered himself flat on his stomach. The pole lay by his side. "I think we're making some kind of record." To himself Ben thought the raft seemed to be going almost too fast. He closed his eyes to let himself feel the rocking motion and listen to the sounds of the choppy waves around them. When he opened them to look for the yellow light on the ship, what he saw was a speck of light in the great dark closet around them.

"Guess we'll make it out to her and back okay," he said. "I'd sure like something to prove we've been right up to her."

Zack's laughter always took a long time finishing as it did now. It seemed to come from deep down to make its way all through him. "I'd like to see Jake Sorley's face when he finds out. Maybe we can come by her anchor rope and find something."

Ben was beginning to worry. If the wind kept rising they would have to turn back.

"Hey, Ben, I can't see nothin' out there. You see somethin'?" Zack called.

Only minutes ago Ben had seen the warship's light. He looked in vain for it now. "She's out there somewhere," he said hopefully. Rain began to fall, pelting them with its force. Ben pulled himself upright. The river could change quickly in a sudden storm, and Ben knew it. Then suddenly it was pouring hard. The wind had become a gale that tossed the raft wildly. The storm broke upon them in fury. "Got to pole us in to shore," Zack shouted.

Ben peered through curtains of blowing rain. Where was the shore? "I can't see anything," he yelled. His face streamed with sheets of water. Zack had crawled over to Ben's side and was trying in vain to light the lantern. There was no place to shield it from wind and rain. Again and again Zack lost his balance as he tried to light it. "Ain't no use," he cried.

Ben's poling too was useless. The strong river current gripped the raft. Wherever they were heading, they were going there fast.

Ben thought he saw a light from the warship, then lost sight of it. There was nothing to do but hold on, anyway. "Must have gone right past the *Eagle*," he shouted. Zack didn't answer. The raft moved swiftly. It dipped and rose on the waves like a wild thing. Suddenly it tipped dangerously. In a minute Ben was soaked to the skin as a wave rushed over them.

He clung to the boards and shouted into the wind, "She's caught! Hold on." With his face pressed against the rough wood all he could do was pray for the Lord's help. Storms on the Hudson River could be quick and deadly. Flat beside him, Zack had flung an arm across him.

"Ben," he cried, "your pa being a preacher, you don't believe old African ways, but Granny sewed powerful medicine in this here rag 'round my neck. A body can't drown if he's wearin' it." Zack grasped

Ben's arm tightly. "You hold on, Ben, you hear?"

Zack's words were drowned in the sudden loud crack of the crash that shivered their raft. Ben felt himself tossed forward. Pain shot up his leg as he spun in a whirl of water and flying sticks. With a thud his rolling body smacked against hard ground.

His mouth felt full of dirt. He spat and opened his eyes. "Zack!" he called.

The arm across Ben was Zack's. It moved off now as Zack pushed himself to his knees. His body rocked back and forth. "Close as I ever been. You hear that crack? Sound like the world comin' to an end."

Ben felt the wet ground under his hands and whispered, "Thank you, Lord, thank you." Aloud he said slowly, "She sure cracked this time. We must've hit a rock." Waves slapped against the sides of the narrow spit of rocky land on which they had landed. "Reckon we won't get to the *Eagle* tonight," he said. He rolled onto his side when a sharp, shooting pain in his left leg forced him back quickly. He groaned out loud and held the throbbing leg tightly. "My leg hurts awful bad," he cried.

"Maybe you done broke it, Ben. Can you move your toes?" Ben did not want to move an inch, but he finally slid one hand slowly down the leg. As it neared the ankle, hot signals of pain rushed up the leg. He let go quickly, brushing against something hard just above the ankle.

His voice rose shrilly. "There's a hunk of wood or something in me."

"Easy now, Ben." Zack's voice came soothing the way it did when he spoke to the horses at Mistress Capp's. "Let me see." Zack's hand felt Ben's clasped ones holding the injured leg.

"Get it out, Zack," Ben pleaded. His voice was shaking, his throat and stomach tight with a sick feeling.

"Easy now, easy." Zack gentled Ben with his voice, while his hands carefully felt the hard piece of stick above Ben's ankle. The stick was as thick as an arrow, sharp at one end like a huge splinter. Carefully Zack curled one hand around the rough wood and the other gently around Ben's foot. Quickly he tightened his hold on the foot and yanked the wood free. Though it was thick the wood had not gone deeply and came out easily.

Ben yelled, but relief came almost at once. His leg still hurt, only now he could move it freely.

Zack rubbed his hand against his wet shirt. "It's bleedin', Ben. Knew it would. Got to tie it up with somethin'. Mistress Capp say this shirt too old anyhow," he said ripping his shirt sleeve free at the shoulder. Feeling for the wound, Zack made a wad of the sleeve and pressed it hard against the oozing wetness. "Hold your hand on that," he ordered. "Got to bind it on tight." He tore the other shirt sleeve and tied its length around the bandage.

"Thank you kindly, Zack. I'm beholding to you."

"Ain't nothin'. Reckon that's two you owe me," Zack said cheerfully.

"What two?" Ben asked as he stood up and slowly tried the injured leg.

"I told you before," Zack insisted. "I reckon Granny's medicine save us both from drownin'."

"No, it didn't," Ben declared. "Just before we hit I asked the Lord to save us both."

"Ain't no way you kin prove it wasn't Granny's medicine," Zack said.

"Come on, Zack, I can't stand here all night arguing with you. We don't even know where we're at." The rain continued to pour down and closed them in like a wall.

As he listened Ben could hear the water slapping against the land around them. "Must be on a spit of land like Bailey's Point. You reckon we got that far, Zack?"

"Maybe," Zack answered. "If we go slow away from the river we'll find the railroad tracks."

"That's right. We can follow the dirt road by the tracks back. Whatever's left of the raft will have to wait till morning. Guess the lantern's gone for good."

They had found the tracks, but it was slow going in the rain and dark. The dirt road next to the tracks churned into mud as they walked. After what seemed like an hour to Ben, whose leg had began to hurt, the rain stopped as suddenly as it had started. The moon appeared from behind the clouds and brought light enough to make their way easier.

Endless dark woods went in either direction along one edge of the tracks, the river on the other.

The night sounds of toads called in the dripping trees. To their left the swollen river slapped against its banks. It was hot again, and the July night seemed to come alive around them. Both boys were familiar with the scolding cries, the scuffling noises of small animals out to feed. The railroad tracks were a sort of no-man's-land, and Ben felt safer by them. He wished they had Zack's old hunting rifle along.

"Zack, I need to fix the bandage on this leg a minute," he called, stopping to sit.

"That bandage slippin'?" Zack asked.

"I just need to tighten it. I think it's stopped bleeding. Wouldn't hurt to have a walking stick, though."

Zack crossed the tracks over to the edge of the woods. "Ought to be somethin' good here," he called back. He returned with a stout branch about the right height for Ben.

Carefully Ben tested the cane's strength. "That's fine, Zack, just right."

As they walked Zack asked, "What you plan to tell your ma?"

"Well," Ben said slowly, "I guess she'll miss the lantern. I ain't thought on it much yet." First he had to try to think where they were.

"Ben," Zack said as if he had been wondering the same thing, "Bailey's Point ain't far from Old Man Bleeker's place. You reckon we're near his place?"

"Could have been Bailey's Point we struck the way we were moving, though it's a mighty long way downriver. If it was, we ought to be somewhere near Bleeker's. By day you can see it from the river sort of off by itself with trees all around."

"You hear what folks say about Old Man Bleeker?" Zack asked. "Say he just turn the key in the door and took off when his missus died. Left everythin' just like that. Ain't nobody been livin' there for years."

"Seems a waste," Ben added, "just leaving a big old house like that to sit empty all this time."

"Ben, you reckon he left his boat layin' up somewhere? Figure it'd be okay to borrow his old boat maybe? It sure would save us a lot of walkin' tonight. We could bring it back soon's we could. Ought to see what we can find left of that raft too."

Ben wished they were back on the river, just gliding along. Since the crash he was beginning to feel bruised and sore in a number of places. "I don't know, Zack. It ain't exactly right. I never properly met Old Man Bleeker."

"So how you know he wouldn't jus' say, 'Why sure, Master Able, you jus' borrow this here boat and get yourself straight home'?"

"Come on, Zack. Likely if he didn't shoot us first for trespassing he'd see we got home, all right, to a whipping for roaming his woods this time of night."

"Maybe so," Zack agreed. "But how he gonna catch us now when he ain't there? Nobody there. Poor old boat jus' sittin' to feel that river again." Zack laughed. "I kin see it now, waitin' for us."

"Maybe it is and maybe it ain't," Ben said stopping to wave away a bunch of gnats. If they did find Bleeker's boat, at least the gnats would not follow them on the river.

The tracks seemed to curve farther away from the river now. On both sides the trees grew thick. Zack stopped walking and stared at the woods to his left. "Ben, this could be Old Man Bleeker's place. There's somethin' over there." He pointed in the direction of the river. "Looks mighty like a road going through those trees."

Ben stared into the shadows. "If you're right, I remember the house is close down by the water." Pushing his way through the undergrowth he walked toward the trees and the deep shadows within. Zack followed. As they drew nearer in the pale moonlight, they saw the wide drive.

Tangled bushes and vines grew wild along what must have been gardens lining the drive that led to the house. In the shadows the house loomed dark and deserted before them.

"It's the Bleeker place, all right," Ben said in a hushed voice.

"Then the dock be round back, and maybe that boat too," Zack whispered. Together they walked slowly, warily toward the house. Nothing stirred. Its upper floor rose into blackness under a slanting roof; its shuttered windows were dark. Zack hurried ahead toward the river to find the dock. By the time Ben reached it Zack had found the boat. Only it was not beached the way Ben thought they would find it. Moored by a rope to the dock, it lay rocking gently on the water. Even the oars were still there, as though left that way only a short while instead of the years since Old Man Bleeker had been gone from the place.

5

Kidnapped

While Ben watched, Zack bent over the boat's mooring rope to undo its knots. Suddenly both boys froze in panic at the sound of galloping horses headed their way. Zack jumped from the dock and ran to the nearest bush. Ben followed quickly and in his hurry forgot the stick in his hand. As he leaped from the edge of the dock, the stick caught between two loose boards, surprising him so that he stumbled and fell. In a flash he was up, crashed into the bushes, and crouched breathlessly beside Zack. The horses had stopped at the house.

Peering out, Ben saw two men, one of them carrying a lantern, come around the corner of the house toward the dock. Beside him Zack bent lower, and Ben did the same, hoping his loudly beating heart would not give them away.

They were several yards away from Ben and Zack's hiding place when the man with the lantern stood still. He was a large man dressed in the working clothes of a laborer or farmer. His voice was gruff as he said, "Now, what might that be thrashing around here this time of night?"

The man next to him was muffled in a long cape and wide-brimmed hat in spite of the hot July night. "Nothing here, John," the capped man said. There was something familiar in his voice. In a flash it came to Ben. It was the same light, clear voice he had heard under the carriage in New York City!

"Must have been a large raccoon or the like," the familiar voice said. "Better take a look, anyway." The two began to look on either side of the path. The one called John went to the dock, swung his lantern above the boat, then bent down and brought the lantern close to examine the ground. He continued to stare at the ground in front of him. Then, as if he knew exactly where to go, he strode directly to the bushes where Ben and Zack crouched. With his pistol pointed straight at the boys, he motioned them to stand up.

"I've found our raccoons, sir, and a sorrier sight I've yet to see. Left your calling card, did you, lad?" The man pointed to Ben's stick, which lay flat at the edge of the dock. "And your tracks in this mud are as fresh and fine as my own. What be your name, lad, and what are you doing sneaking about here?"

Fear gripped Ben so hard he could scarcely swallow. "Ben Able, sir," he whispered.

"And you, boy, are you a runaway, now? Be ye North or South, boy?" The stranger took a firm grip on Zack's shoulder.

Zack's voice sounded froggy. "I ain't never been south. Ain't no runaway, sir."

"And what were you doing down here?" the man demanded, shaking Zack's shoulder.

"Ain't doin' nothin', sir," Zack answered. "We jus' gettin' along home now. Done busted our raft on that ole river. We sure jus' goin' on home, sir."

"This is a fine mess," the caped man said as he came over to look at Zack and Ben. He peered in the direction of the river. "There's the signal light now. Better get that boat untied while I watch these two. We've no time to waste."

"Aye, sir, it won't take but a minute." Taking the lantern with him, he left.

Ben was positive now that the caped man was one of the two mystery men he had heard talking in New York City, but the one called John had an accent Ben was sure he had not heard under the carriage.

In the dim light the silver-worked handle of the pistol gleamed in the caped man's hand. Ben couldn't take his eyes from the gun. Who was this man, and what was that about a signal light? A southern spy flashed through his mind. Was he only dreaming all this? His thoughts were interrupted by the return of the other stranger.

"We have no choice but to take these two, John. There's no telling what they've seen or heard. They might have gotten inside the house. Bring them along. We can't leave them here, and we must go at once."

"You're lucky, lads," John whispered. He leered at Ben and Zack as he hurried them toward the dock. "If I had me way, you'd both be in the river and out of me way. Course, you might still fetch a pretty penny," he added, pushing his pistol against Zack's shoulder. "Move along, now."

Though he knew his heart was beating loudly, Ben felt dazed, as if he were dreaming. The man in the cape reached a hand to help him into the boat. At John's prodding Zack climbed in next to Ben. If it was a dream that he and Zack were being kidnapped, he wished he could wake up. The man in the cape sat huddled in the prow of the boat as the other rowed them away from shore.

Clouds had moved in to cover the moon. Ben strained to see in the darkness. Were they going across to the other side? The warship was nowhere in sight. Cold gripped him, making him shiver as if it were a fall night. He pressed his body close to Zack's for warmth.

The words "You'll fetch a pretty penny" rang in his head. Did they mean to sell Zack to some farmer in spite of the fact it was illegal? Or worse, smuggle him into the hands of some southern owner? What would they do with him? At least now they were together. If they separated them, what then? Ben's heart thumped so loudly he wondered if Zack could hear it. "Please Lord," he prayed silently, "please help us. Don't let them sell Zack." In his heart he repeated "What time I am afraid, I will trust in thee."

Zack clutched the red rag around his neck. In a hushed voice he whispered, "I got Granny's charm, Ben. You stay by me."

"Not a word, lads," John hissed, "or I'll knock your heads in."

Zack sat up straighter. His mouth closed firmly. Ben clamped his own lips tightly together. He could feel his teeth chattering.

When the boat neared midstream, Ben saw John lower the anchor into the river, then pick up the lantern and swing it from side to side. Slowly the signal light blinked in answer. As the light came toward them, the shadowy shape of a small steamer came into sight. She was running with only the single light.

For a second Ben thought it was the *Mary Queen*, but it could not be she in the middle of the night. The *Mary Queen* made her runs at exactly the same time each day. He and Zack knew just when she would be coming into the Requia dock in Tarrytown. Her big, beautiful paddle wheel would slow, and Captain Merry would be standing proudly on deck.

The boat's engine cut. Now Ben could plainly see her drifting close to them. She was bigger than he had first thought, but no different from the boats that came up the river past Tarrytown almost daily.

The boat drew close enough for one of the crew to lower its ropes. Quickly the caped man climbed aboard. Almost instantly, Ben felt himself lifted clear of the side onto the ropes. Above him rough hands pulled him onto the deck. In a moment Zack landed beside him. Glancing back quickly, Ben saw Old Man Bleeker's boat already heading back to shore. He gritted his teeth to keep his mouth from trembling. He knew for certain he and Zack were in real trouble.

The single light showed little of the deck, hardly more than the sketchy outlines of fishing rig, a deck cabin, and the hatch.

"Take those two below and stow them," ordered the man who stood talking with the caped stranger.

"Aye, sir!" One of the crew snapped into action and grabbed Ben and Zack by the shoulders with his large, powerful hands. He let go only to shove them ahead down the hatch. A small lantern hung from the ceiling showed cupboards lining the walls, a tiny kitchen with a table, stools, and storage area. Zack and Ben were shoved toward bunk beds built into the walls and ordered to stay put. The fierce scowl of the brawny sailor towering over them threatened more than words. As he left he took the lantern. With a heavy thud the hatch closed behind him. The boys were in complete darkness.

Ben felt cold inside him in spite of the fact that Zack's warm body was close beside.

"'Spect we got real trouble," Zack whispered. "You think we locked in here, Ben?"

"I can't tell. It's too dark in here to see a thing," Ben answered, keeping his voice low.

"We got to get out of here. Whoever they be, they mean no good," Zack added.

Ben thought of all the spy stories filling the newspapers these days: Rebel Rose of Washington, Sandford the Confederate telegraph spy, and Mr. Pinkerton who worked for President Lincoln. "I think I know one of them," he answered. Quickly he told Zack about the conversation he had overheard under the carriage in New York City. "They sure don't want anybody looking inside the Bleeker house, whatever the reason is."

"Reckon this boat could be part of their smuggling plan," Zack said. "And that's why we be headin' north. We need to get us out of here fast."

Zack was right. They were going north. Or were they? "You sure about that, Zack? How do you know we ain't heading down to New York City?"

"Think on it, Ben. When we come on board, this boat going north, right? She ain't turned 'round since, has she?"

Zack was right again. "Guess we'd have felt her turning," Ben admitted. The heavy smell of the stale air below deck made his head ache. It seemed like a long time since they had crashed the raft.

Zack had risen from the bunk. Ben could hear him thumping on the walls. "What are you doing, Zack?" he asked anxiously.

"Trying to find that ladder so I can reach the hatch." Ben heard more thumping and then silence. "I found the hatch, but it's shut good." Zack's voice came out of the dark. "We got trouble. Ain't no way out of here but that hatch."

"Okay, Zack, we have to think of something else. Maybe when they come for us we can jump overboard and swim to shore." Ben kept talking until Zack stumbled onto the bunk beside him.

"Maybe we got to swim across the river," Zack agreed. "We got to be ready first chance we get. Sure somethin' bad goin' on here."

Ben was trying to stay awake but his head, which leaned against the cabin's hard wooden wall, kept slipping sideways. Zack sounded farther and farther away.

Ben jerked awake. His neck was stiff and sore from the awkward position he had fallen into. Daylight was coming through the cracks in the slightly opened hatch. As Ben blinked his eyes in an effort to remember where he was, it suddenly rushed back to him. He and Zack were being kidnapped right on their own river.

The sleeping Zack lay in a heap with his arms and legs curled into a corner of the bunk. Ben was about to awaken him when he saw that they were not alone. The caped man lay asleep on a bunk on the opposite wall. Ben could see the pistol stuffed into the man's waistband. With a shock he saw the man's face.

In the light he was certain. This was the same young man with the black satchel who had boarded the coach in New York City the day the riots began! The narrow face, the shapely mouth, the chin, the light gold hair were unmistakable. Under different circumstances, Ben would have thought the face to be a fair one, even a kind one. The voice Ben had heard under the carriage plotting to help the South belonged to the very same man who had ridden in the coach with Ben and his father to Tarrytown!

Quietly he reached out and gently shook Zack. Zack started up, and Ben clapped a hand over his mouth. He pointed to the sleeping man across the way. Zack's eyes grew big for a moment. Slowly Ben dropped his hand.

Carefully he lowered his feet over the side of the bunk. Zack did the same. Both were standing when a loud knock sounded on the hatch.

The gentleman across from them groaned, sat up, stretched, and looked at the boys. "I take it we have arrived," he said as he stood. His cornflower-blue eyes looked disapprovingly at Ben and Zack. "Babes," he said disgustedly.

From the deck a voice called roughly, "Get a move on, down there."

A chill ran down Ben's back. He looked at Zack, who nodded, as if to remind him to be ready the minute they could jump. He nodded back.

On deck the early morning air was cool. The fishing boat had pulled in close to shore. A small boat floated alongside. Its rower, a gray-haired man with a red handkerchief around his neck, sat waiting.

Before Ben could think clearly, he and Zack were being herded over the side into the waiting boat. The young man followed and tossed his black bag ahead of him. He had taken off his cape, and Ben noted the pistol still in his waistband. Would he shoot if they jumped? They would never make it, anyway, with the other boat still nearby to point them out to these two. The man with the handkerchief around his neck could probably row faster than he and Zack could swim. He shook his head slightly as Zack looked questioningly at him. Then, pretending to cough, he covered his mouth with his hand and whispered, "Not now." Zack nodded.

The river was narrower here than at Tarrytown, its banks heavily wooded. Ben could see nothing familiar. They were somewhere between towns. Not a house or a landmark showed anywhere, nothing but miles of thickly wooded slopes.

"I'll be taking you straight to the General's," the old man said. "Weren't expecting these two." He pointed at Zack and Ben. "I'll explain to the General," their captor said as he settled himself. The old man rowed the boat into a small cove that was hidden by trees that grew on both sides. He held it steady while they climbed out. They waited while he dragged the boat ashore into a patch of bushes. In a few minutes it was completely hidden under a pile of loose branches.

The young man put Ben and Zack ahead of himself and behind the old man. Ben heard Zack beside him mumble, "Big trouble."

It was a rough trail, hardly worth calling a trail. Ben knocked his sore leg several times against large tree roots. In spite of the trouble they were in, his stomach reminded him noisily how empty it was. The path grew steeper as they continued. Thick woods hemmed them in on all sides. Zack grabbed a young tree to steady himself and Ben did the same. Large uneven boulders underfoot made the climb worse. Ben was sweating now, but inside something cold still clutched him. Who were these men, and where were they taking Zack and him? By now half of Tarrytown would know the two of them were missing. But how would anyone ever find them? Ben's heart sank.

6

A Nest of Vipers

The ground had begun to level off, though Ben and the others were still walking through dense woods. Ben nearly bumped into Zack when at last they stepped into an enormous clearing. In front of them, cold and huge, unfriendly even in the morning light, loomed a mansion like none Ben had ever seen. Its massive dark stone walls looked more than anything like those of some ancient fort. Many of the windows on each of its three stories were tightly shuttered. On the roof a low wall ran across the length, and behind it a small, boxlike tower rose still higher. It looked something like the captain's walks built on top of several large homes along the river from which people spotted incoming ships. But what would anyone want with a lookout this far upriver? Beside him Zack whispered, "Looks mighty old to me."

"Right. Can't think who'd be living here now," Ben whispered back.

Their young captor motioned Ben and Zack to move ahead. As his eyes caught Ben's, Ben saw a fleeting look of softness, almost a sorry look. The man turned his face away and moved ahead of them to the heavy wooden door. "Take them around back to the kitchen. I'm sure the cook can put them to work. You'd best tell him to keep an eye on them till I've time to see to them." The door had opened to admit him when he called back and added, "And have someone take a look at the boy's leg."

"It's on with you, now," the old man said and pushed the boys toward the back of the house. "My stomach's empty as a March hare's. Hurry up, or you'll feel my hand."

Ben and Zack quickened their steps to escape the man's big hands. At the back of the mansion several men came and went from the nearby stables. Everywhere there was noise and activity, some of it from the chickens and pigs that roamed the yard. "Where'd you pick them two up?" a man cleaning a gun called out. "You recruiting, or you plan on selling them?" Ben felt his stomach churn. Zack lowered his eyes.

"Never you mind," the old man retorted. "I 'spect the General will know what to do with them." Roughly he pushed both boys ahead through a small arched doorway. They had come out of the bright sunlight into a large, gloomy room with a massive stove and wooden table. It was clearly the kitchen area. A short Chinese man wearing a black cap on his head looked up in surprise as they entered.

With a hand on each of their necks, the old man forced Zack and Ben to sit on one of the wooden benches at the table. "Now, Cookie, you are to keep these two like they was the last chickens on earth.

You can put 'em to work, but they'd better be here when the General calls, you hear?"

"Yes suh, yes suh, Sing hear good." The little cook half bowed as he answered. With each bow his long black pigtail bobbed up and down with him.

As the old man stomped out of the kitchen the young caped man came in and sat on the other bench. He rested his head on one arm and spoke wearily to the cook. "Mr. Sing, these boys are in my care for the moment. Please see that they have food. Since the General will not arrive till later this afternoon, I will be in the guest room. I should like my meal sent up. You may leave it by my door." He stood up to leave. "Oh, and can you do something for the boy's leg?"

"Sing can do everything, young gentleman," the cook said. His smile showed yellow teeth with a dark gap in front where two were missing. He bowed as before, then turned to the monstrous fireplace.

Zack whispered to Ben, "You reckon we're in a Confederate fort or somethin'?" Zack looked worried. Ben frowned. How could a southern fort be so far north? The Confederates, as the southern states called themselves, might have a secret hideaway this far, but he doubted it was a fort. Besides, they had seen no big guns. The plot he had overheard in New York City somehow was coming together, and they were caught in the middle.

His thoughts were interrupted as Sing, the cook,

plunked down two wooden bowls of thick, greasy soup. Too hungry to waste time worrying about the taste, Ben ate quickly and finished the last drop just as Zack put down his empty bowl. Whatever the flavor was, it tasted better than Ben had expected. The weak beer Sing handed them in huge mugs made his mouth pucker. But Zack seemed not to notice the bitterness. Quickly Ben swallowed the rest.

"Sing make good medicine. Fix everything," the cook said. He pulled Ben's bandaged leg onto the bench.

"Never mind. I'd rather you didn't bother," Ben protested and looked to Zack for help. Zack shrugged his shoulders. Ben winced as the cook pulled off the dry, filthy bandage that had once been Zack's shirtsleeves. With a strong grip on Ben's leg, he proceeded to wash the cut.

"Now Sing put on medicine. You see tomorrow everything better." The yellow paste he applied smelled strong enough to make Ben turn away. "You good as new," the cook declared as he tied a fresh rag around Ben's leg. When he was finished, he stood with his hands on his hips and called, "Trim, you come here now. Trim?"

Slowly, a boy a few years older than Ben and Zack stumbled from behind the great chimney. Ben watched him with narrowed eyes. Something in the boy's expressionless face seemed odd.

"Trim, you watch boys. You watch 'em good for Sing. You show boys what to do. Sing need lotsa help around here." The cook turned to Ben and Zack and, raising his large butcher knife to his throat, made a gesture that caused a shiver along Ben's spine. "You boys run away, Sing find you; slit throat like chicken."

The boy called Trim shuffled toward Ben and Zack. Neither of them moved. His mouth opened to speak, but what came out was an explosion of sputtered, jumbled sounds that were meaningless to them. Ben stared at the boy's face and searched his large dark eyes, but they told him nothing. Zack, as puzzled as he, shook his head slightly.

Trim gestured for the boys to come. Ben gave a meaningful look at Zack and then followed the boy out into the courtyard. Behind him, Zack whispered softly, "Somethin' wrong with that boy, Ben. Granny say he be born in a full moon, too soon, an accident."

Ben knew that his father would say, "The Creator has his own reasons, and one day, we will know." "Please help us get safely out of here," Ben prayed again. The terrible fear was beginning to loosen its cold grip on his body, but he was still scared. Nothing like this had ever happened before. Like a voice in his heart he heard the words "What time I am afraid I will put my trust in thee."

Trim led them into the woods a short way, still in sight of the clearing, where a small spring flowed. He made them understand by his slow and deliberate motions that they were to fill the buckets he had brought. After that they worked in a part of the garden weeding. At one point Trim led them to a spot overgrown by weeds that looked as if it had once been a large garden area. At times his hands moved wildly, jerking as though he could not control them. With great effort he pushed through a thicket of bushes to a small, crude hutch. Inside were three baby rabbits. Spluttering, Trim made unintelligible sounds.

Zack knelt by the hutch. "Them's your rabbits, Trim?" he said softly. "Reckon their mamma got herself killed, and you been taking care of them?" Trim nodded vigorously in agreement.

"You doin' a mighty good job, Trim," Zack said, still speaking softly.

Ben crouched on the ground and held a bit of grass through the wire. The rabbits came eagerly to nibble at it. Ben smiled up at Trim. "They're healthy little things."

A soft light came into Trim's eyes as he looked at the rabbits. He looked back at Ben and then at Zack as if deciding something. He made a noise and motioned for them to follow and led them to an old maple tree at the far end of the underbrush.

Partway up the tree trunk was a large dark hollow with a stick nailed at its edge to form a perch. From inside his shirt Trim produced a small sack and shook a handful of seeds into the opening in the tree. In a moment the dark head of a young raven appeared to peck at the seed. Trim waited till the bird had eaten some, then with trembling hands he reached for the bird and lifted him from the hole.

The bird's left wing was badly torn, and one foot had been crushed beyond healing. Trim held the bird close, murmuring to it, then placed it on the perch. While Ben and Zack watched he pulled out a tin lid and refilled it with water from the rusty canteen he wore on his belt.

Zack bent to pull up handfuls of soft grass and held them up to Trim. "This grass'll make his nest nice and fresh."

Trim smiled. Reaching inside the tree once more he swept out handfuls of dry grass and replaced them with the fresh ones from Zack. With the water and fresh seed, Trim seemed satisfied. While they watched, the bird hobbled its way back into the tree nest.

"Trim, that bird owes his life to you. That leg of his and that wing look like he caught a bullet. You doing a good job of doctorin'." Zack smiled broadly at Trim.

Ben knew how good Zack was with hurt animals. Like Zack, the boy Trim seemed to have a way with them too.

There was something Trim was trying to tell them now. His eyes darted anxiously from the tree back toward the rabbit hutch, and his hands waved wildly.

Zack spoke softly. "Trim, you trying to say you don't want anyone to know 'bout this place or the rabbits' hutch?" Trim nodded his head up and down violently. "Don't you worry none," Zack said. "Ben and me just want to be friends. You can count on us."

"Right," Ben added. "Your secret is safe with us, Trim."

They spent the rest of the day working. Sing worked hard to prepare the meals. Ben had counted at least a dozen men at the rough table set up outside the kitchen door. Someone ate in the mansion's dining room, but neither Ben nor Zack was allowed behind its massive doors. Sing himself took the trays of food inside, and from the looks of the heaped up bowls and platters, Ben knew they were meant for more than one person.

The supper meal of cold foods and ale came at last. After they had fetched buckets and buckets of water from the spring and scrubbed mountains of greasy pots, Sing finally told Trim to take the boys to his room for the night. "You watch them good," he ordered Trim.

The room where Trim slept was at the opposite end of the house away from the kitchen. A straw mat and blanket lay on the floor. Trim motioned Ben and Zack to the far corner of the room away from the door and made signs that they were to lie down on the floor. He watched as Ben slid down with his back against the wall and as Zack did the same. With strong motions of his large hands Trim made them understand they were to lie down flat on the floor. With a sigh Zack lay flat, and Ben followed. Finally satisfied, Trim lay down on his straw bed between the boys and the door. With a puff of air he blew out the single candle Sing had given him.

The upper half of the window in the room was unshuttered, as if someone had broken the shutter in two, leaving the lower half in place. Moonlight streamed in the window, and high above, stars gleamed brightly. Ben was so tired even the hard floor felt good to him. Strangely enough, Trim had fallen asleep almost instantly, for now his breathing was deep and regular. Ben had the uneasy feeling that if he and Zack should try to get out of the room Trim could awaken as easily as he had fallen asleep.

He whispered, "You asleep, Zack?"

"Ain't sleepin'. Wonder what they be plannin' to do with us. What we got to do is get out of here. You thinkin' how we be leavin' here?"

Ben thought a second and answered, "Reckon we'll have to make a run for it to the river, cross over, and stay under cover till we reach a town." He listened for Trim's regular breathing. It continued as before. "You see how Trim lifted those iron pots, water and all? He's strong as an ox, even if he is friendly. Sure is a strange one. Can't talk, can't hardly walk right, but I got a feeling he knows a lot. The thing is, he seems to listen to Sing. If Sing told him to keep an eye on us, I reckon Trim will do just that."

Zack grunted. "Maybe he'd help us, and maybe he wouldn't. Guess we best be plannin' without him."

"I think he's harmless, but Sing did tell him to watch us. He might not mean harm, just mean to stop us." Ben thought of the kick one rough-looking man had given Trim. Trim had simply stood still and then moved slowly out of the man's way.

Zack interrupted his thoughts. "Ben, who you think the General be?" All day the boys had heard men use that name—the General.

"We know he's running supplies down from Canada by way of Lake Champlain, through the canal, and onto the Hudson River straight to New York City. Has to be that route. But maybe he is a real Confederate general, and for all we know this could be a secret Confederate headquarters," Ben said. There were plenty of rumors these days about a secret army of southern supporters being raised right in the North. Maybe this was it.

"How close you think we be to Canada?" Zack asked. Canada was supposed to be neutral, which meant it did not take either the North's side in the war or the South's side. But the newspapers said it was more sympathetic to the South, and many southern prisoners who escaped made their way into Canada. The most famous copperhead, Vallandigham, had his headquarters in Canada.

"The river doesn't run up that far. Still, we might be close to where it hits the canal. One thing's certain, we're not near any towns. Listen, Zack, whatever it is that's going on here, maybe we can find out. You game for staying on here at least until tomorrow to see what we can find?"

There was silence. Then Zack whispered, "I suppose old Granny can do without me one more day. The way that Trim is sleeping I reckon we can jus' walk out of here when we're ready. One good thing, ain't no dogs here to give us away." Now that Zack mentioned it, Ben hadn't seen any dogs either. "We know we have to go downhill to get to the river," Zack continued. "Know too where the old man hid that boat. Guess we be needin' a candle and a good head start."

"Right," Ben agreed. Tomorrow they would look sharply at everything.

In the morning, Sing greeted the boys with an angry banging of pots onto the wooden table. "Sing got enough trouble. Now he got to make fuss for big boss visitor." He grabbed handfuls of greens to throw into the pots as he talked. Trim motioned to the boys to pick up the water buckets and follow him.

By mealtime wild turkey, stuffed and roasted, stood near platters of rabbit in sauce and several large river bass. Clams, surrounded by July cucumbers, radishes, and scallions, were piled high. Sing threw the last bit of green herbs into the soup. Ben stood nervously next to Zack. They were to serve in the General's private dining room.

7

A Lady Spy

The great dining hall, grand as it must once have been, looked bare and cold to Ben. The very air of the room felt damp with age as he listened to Sing's instructions on serving. Dark velvet drapes, heavy with a musty odor, hung at the tall narrow window. Years of decay clung to the faded walls and cracked tiles of the floor. A long, dark wooden table and chairs stood in the center of the room. On one wall a giant sideboard with carved claw-footed legs held plates and tarnished silver utensils. One end of the table was set for five. Once more Sing motioned with his ever present butcher knife to silence the boys' protests. Ben and Zack would serve or else.

When the dining room bell rang for service Zack looked grim as he clutched the wine he was to pour. Ben's hands shook so that the soup in the large bowl he carried slopped dangerously close to spilling. Sing pushed Zack ahead into the dining room and prodded Ben to follow.

At the head of the table sat a short, stout man. Ben knew he had to be the General. Two of the General's men sat on either side of him, and next to one of them was the young man who had kidnapped Ben and Zack. The chair in front of the fifth place was empty. Their captor had changed his traveler's clothes for a gentleman's dress coat. His light gold hair was smoothed back neatly.

The General's nearly bald head was bent over a paper in front of him. Trembling, Ben took the soup and held it out. As the General lifted his head, Ben stared. A jagged scar ran from the man's forehead to his black beard. "Hold steady, boy," he growled at Ben. His dark, deeply set eyes were cold as a snake's. With one large hand the General gripped the shaking soup bowl and helped himself.

Somehow Ben managed to walk around the table till the others had helped themselves. No one paid attention to him or Zack as they served. Only the young man paused long enough to look searchingly into Ben's eyes before returning to the conversation. Behind Ben, Zack poured wine. From the corner of his eye Ben saw that Zack's hands were shaking too.

The boys were about to serve Sing's next course of turkey and wild rabbit when the fifth guest arrived. Immediately the General and his men rose. The man who entered the dining hall was well dressed and handsome. His smile flashed below a carefully cut mustache. Every inch of him from his shining boots to his head was that of a gentleman. When he spoke his voice had a pleasant, soft southern drawl.

"Please be seated, gentlemen," he said.

The General swept one large hand toward the golden haired young man. "Mr. Ames, Mr. Jackson," he said introducing the newcomer. Mr. Jackson bowed slightly and took his seat.

So their kidnapper's name was Mr. Ames. Ben noticed a flush of red pass across Mr. Ames's face. Then he was too busy to think of anything but the continual handing around of platters between trips to the kitchen.

The final dish had been served, and all that remained was the refilling of wine glasses. Ben stood close to the wall half-hidden in the shadow of the heavy window drapes. Zack finished pouring wine, then quietly joined him. The men, deep in conversation, seemed to have forgotten their presence. Sing and Trim were either in the kitchen or outside feeding the rest of the General's men. Ben supposed he and Zack should leave the room, but one part of him wanted to stay and listen to what their captor was saying to the man called Jackson.

"Mr. Jackson," the young man said, "I trust your trip to Canada was successful?"

"It was indeed, Mr. Ames," he answered. "My business contacts were most agreeable. By the time tonight's shipment arrives another should already be leaving Canada."

"You do not travel with your cargo then, sir?" Mr. Ames asked.

Mr. Jackson laughed before he replied. "It would not do to risk too much, sir. My captains are well paid for the risk they take."

"Sir," Mr. Ames said, "my contacts are ready and willing to buy your second shipment should it prove satisfactory to our needs. How soon do you expect delivery?"

"That, Mr. Ames, depends, shall we say, on favorable shipping weather. And I daresay the cost of such things as the South requires has gone up. Our captains alone earn three thousand in gold for each trip."

Mr. Ames's voice was angry as he said, "As you may know, Mr. Jackson, you are not the only source of supplies. There are still gallant blockade runners who manage to slip past the North's ships into at least one of our ports. They carry a far greater load and risk much more for the same in gold each trip."

"But, my dear sir, fewer and fewer are able to get through, I fear," Mr. Jackson replied. "The North has sent many good ships to the bottom of the sea. Our way may be costly, what with bribes at both the canal and to New York City's port inspectors, but our suppliers are quite reliable. We shall prove worthy of our price."

"We must hope so, sir," the young man replied. "You are aware, Mr. Jackson, no doubt of the New York draft riots that have turned the city upside down these past few days? I only wish we could have turned the whole of New York against the war."

Mr. Jackson smiled broadly. "What we needed, sir, was a dozen more like yourself, Mr. Ames. Or, should I say, Miss Lila Jorgin?"

A deadly silence descended on the room. The General's hand with his wine glass stopped halfway to his mouth.

The golden haired youth began, "How dare you, sir," his voice shaking slightly.

Mr. Jackson laughed. "Come, come, my dear. You are among friends. Did you expect that I would not have recognized you, the richest little heiress in all of Carolina? You attended the governor's ball. You dance well!" Still smiling, he turned toward the General. "You see, General, how honored we are. Between lands in the South and investments in England, Miss Jorgin owns roughly several millions."

The General gaped at the former Mr. Ames, then threw back his head in loud laughter. "And her dressed like that. A real adventuress. Well, well, this calls for a celebration."

Ames's, rather, Miss Jorgin's face was flushed with anger. "You forget, General Brown, we are fighting a war, any way that we can. I resent being called an adventuress."

The General smiled broadly. "My apology. I should have said lady spy." He laughed again.

Miss Jorgin rose to her feet and held her wine glass high. "Your words are dangerous, sir. I am Miss Jorgin, but more than that, I am a Southerner. I drink to the South and her cause. My fortunes, my lands, my life for hers."

Rising to his feet Mr. Jackson lifted his glass. The General and his men followed quickly. "Hear, hear; well said, my dear. To the South and to all our fortunes joined in hers. We shall do all we can to help her gallant cause." The General chimed in, "Aye, aye, sir," raising his half-empty glass high.

Ben exchanged a look of astonishment with Zack. The youth who had helped to catch them was a woman! Her shortened hair had made it difficult to tell in spite of her soft young face. Her slenderness and graceful movements were like a woman's, now that he noticed.

Miss Jorgin remained standing, then excused herself, and left the room. At that moment Sing entered and pushed Zack toward the table to refill the wine glasses. With the other hand he motioned Ben back into the kitchen with him.

"Sing needed to fix broken leg for foolish man who let horse step on him. You clean up here with Trim." Ben stared at the mountain of dirty plates and greasy pots before him. Trim had already fetched water. As the kitchen door to the yard closed behind Sing, Ben glanced at Trim who was awkwardly washing plates. Moving slowly and quietly Ben made his way to the dining hall door to press his ear against the wood.

The General's loud voice came through clearly. "She'll bring a ransom fit for a queen. What luck!"

"Ah, General," Mr. Jackson answered, "better still, why should we bother ourselves with setting up for a ransom? I have a far less difficult plan in mind. The lady is beautiful and rich. With her fortune added to mine we will be our own little empire."

"You're the boss, sir," the General said. "But I'll wager you you're in for a storm with that one. I'd rather tackle the ransom, myself." Ben heard laughter as he listened. A quick look back at Trim assured him that Trim's mind was still on the dishes before him.

"We shall see what pretty net will snare the pretty hare," Jackson said. "She expects to leave in the morning with the shipment of contraband coming in tonight. I shall tell her the boat has been delayed, and we must be patient. Meanwhile get that cargo on its way to the city as soon as it shows up."

"What's our cover this time?" the General asked.

"Bibles, sir, Bibles," Jackson replied. "You are carrying the powerful Word of the Lord to those poor city people. As usual, there are certain marked crates that contain Bibles for inspection. Your contact is the Reverend Austin Smith. You know the password."

The General raised his voice, "A toast men. Here's to the South that produces the cotton; to the Yankees that maintain the blockade and keep up the price of cotton; and to the Britishers who buy the cotton and pay the high price for it. Three cheers for a long war."

"And," Mr. Jackson added, "long may we sell to both North and South with never a cost to us."

At that moment the door opened flinging Ben backward as Zack came rushing into the kitchen. Sing, too, had returned.

8

An Agreement

All the next day the boys did not see the General, Mr. Jackson, or Miss Jorgin. Sing himself took the covered trays of food into the dining room. Ben and Zack were put to work with Trim cleaning pots, weeding the garden, and a hundred other chores.

After the light evening meal was over and the cleanup through, Sing prepared a special tray of food. He called the boys to him. "Lady not eating. Mr. Jackson say to take her best of everything on best tray. One carry tray, one take humble gift of flowers. Trim knows room for guest on third floor." Ben took Sing's large bouquet of sweet peas, brown-eyed daisies, and wild fern. Zack carried the tray as Trim led the way up a wide sweeping staircase to a landing with three narrow windows above it. The landing divided like a Y into arms that curved up to the hallways of the second floor. The halls were windowless, but in the fading light from the first landing and the candle Trim held, Ben could see several doors leading off to his right. As they climbed the second staircase, sounds of loud laughter came from somewhere down the dark hall. The stairs to the third floor, though still wide and sweeping, went directly to the upper hall. Here Trim turned right again down a long corridor. He stopped at one of the doors, then stepped back and let his hand drop to his side.

Puzzled, Ben was about to say something when the sound of Miss Jorgin's voice rose in anger from inside the room.

"First you hold me here like some common wench. Oh, yes, I heard the *Sheila's* boat whistle. I don't know what game you are playing, sir, but we are at war. I have no time for games. You speak to me of marriage? I am married to the South."

The next voice was clearly Mr. Jackson's. "My dear, I have no idea what you are talking about. You may have heard another boat. There are many that use the river, which is why we chose this forsaken place. It's out of sight, yet we can unload or reload, take on passengers at night without anyone the wiser, thanks to the tunnel that runs from the waterfront to the house. I assure you, my dear, you did not hear the *Sheila*. She is, unfortunately, delayed. You know how those things can be, what with the canal traffic and all."

"No, I do not know, sir," Miss Jorgin said emphatically.

"My dear Lila, I do not play games. I am in earnest. I have every bit as much southern blood in my veins as yourself. You are a beautiful woman, especially when you are angry. I want you as my wife, war or no war. But there's no time to waste, my dear. Think how we will help the cause together."

"Never!" Miss Jorgin's voice rose. "Get out. Do you hear?"

As Jackson's laughter came through to the hallway there was the sound of an object crashing against the door. Miss Jorgin's voice screamed, "How dare you, how dare you! Come near me again and I'll scratch your eyes out."

Zack whispered, "You think we better go on back down?" Before Ben could answer they heard the angry voice of Mr. Jackson.

"You little cat, you've drawn blood!" Instantly his voice changed and became calm. "Forgive me, my dear. I am a man, and your going about dressed the way you are made me forget myself. My apologies. I will not forget again that I am courting the fairest flower of the South." His voice became pleading. "Lila, for the sake of our beloved South, think what it would mean. As my wife no one would ever suspect you of spying. And if you wish, you could leave all of that to me and help our cause at home. We need each other, and the South needs us both." There was no answer from Miss Jorgin.

"Goodnight, then," Jackson said. The door opened and slammed shut as Mr. Jackson came into the hall. He looked angrily at Trim and the boys. "You have the lady's supper?" Lifting the napkin on the tray in Zack's hands, he inspected its contents. "Take it in," he commanded and left. He held a handkerchief to his face. Ben had seen the two long scratches on the man's left cheek.

There was no answer as Trim knocked. Ben called through the door, "Miss Jorgin, we've brought your supper."

The door opened a few inches as Miss Jorgin checked her callers. Her face looked flushed, and Ben thought she would have liked to cry. "You might as well come in," she said and opened the door farther.

She stood aside to let them enter. Ben and Zack went into the room, but Trim stood firmly in the hall.

"He's a shy one, Miss," Zack said quickly.

Miss Jorgin glanced at Trim, smiled, and nodded her head slightly. "Will you wait here, Trim?" she asked gently. Trim nodded his head vigorously. "That's fine, Trim. These two will be with you in just a few minutes." She shut the door, then indicated a table where Ben and Zack could put down their burdens. The boys turned to go.

"Wait," Miss Jorgin said slowly. "I've something to say." She sat on the edge of her bed and looked directly at the two of them. "You know who I am, and you know why I couldn't let you stay in Tarrytown. You must know too that John would not have let you go if I hadn't brought you along." Ben looked at Zack but said nothing. If they had been given over to John, what might have happened made Ben shiver.

"In a while this war will be over," she said. "Believe me, I wish for peace for all of us." She stood up and paced the room. "Whatever you've heard about spies who carry messages and report military secrets, my job is much less romantic. I work to get medicine, food, blankets, and other essentials kept from us by the North's blockade of our ports. And yes, whenever I can I try to get word to some of our captured soldiers in prison here in the North. Yes, I also urge our friends in the North to help us. I do believe some of your generals would hang me for less." She stopped and faced the boys. "Nevertheless, right now you need my help, and I need yours. I have no desire to leave you here. Do you want to get out of here?"

Both boys stared at her. "Yes, ma'am," Ben said, and Zack nodded in agreement.

"Then if you'll help me, I'll help you." Miss Jorgin looked Ben straight in the eyes. Her clear questioning eyes demanded an answer. Ben knew that he would help her get away.

"And you, boy," Miss Jorgin turned to Zack. "Whatever you've heard about the South, we take care of our property. Look at your elbows, and probably your knees, too. When is the last time you greased them?"

Ben looked in surprise at Zack's arms. The elbows were gray, dry, rough. Zack's voice was low and surly. "Ain't no coon fat here." Miss Jorgin took Zack's left arm firmly and led him over to the dressing table. From a small box she took ointment and applied it to Zack's rigid arm around the elbow. Then she did the other one.

"There." She turned away and replaced the ointment on the table. "When is the last time a northern woman did that for you?" Zack said nothing but stood sullenly and stared at the floor.

Ben wondered how much Miss Jorgin really did know about the General and Mr. Jackson's plan. Suddenly he was pouring out all he and Zack had heard the two men planning.

Miss Jorgin listened quietly. "So, I'm a prisoner either for ransom or a forced marriage. I was hoping for more time, but this changes everything." Once more she paced the room. "Still, I promised I'd help you." She faced them with a thoughtful look on her face. "If we make the first move we may be able to surprise them. Can you return here tonight?"

"We can come after Trim falls asleep," Ben said in a hushed voice so that Trim wouldn't hear.

"Good," Miss Jorgin said. "Wait until you are sure the household is asleep." Folding a small white paper she handed it to Ben. "Slip this bit of paper under my door, and I'll open it. Don't knock, don't speak. Everything depends on secrecy. Your own lives depend on it."

Ben tucked the paper into his shirt. A shiver of excitement ran through him as Miss Jorgin led them to the door to let them out. Trim stood waiting where they had left him. The candle in his hand still burned. When he saw them he turned toward the stairs and without a word led them back the way they had come.

9

The Dungeon

Through the unshuttered half of the window the moon shone brightly on Trim's straw mat. He had fallen asleep almost at once. "At least we'll have moonlight once we're outside," Ben thought. He stared at Trim's sleeping form lying on the mat. They would have to get past him first and into the hall, make their way up to Miss Jorgin's room then back down the stairs. Once they were outside they would head toward the river, uncover the small boat, and be off.

He tried to picture Miss Jorgin as a southern spy but failed. She was a prisoner, the same as he and Zack. None of them were safe in the General's hands or Jackson's.

Still, it was against the law to help the South, and she belonged to the enemy side. She had kidnapped them. On the other hand, she could have left them behind with John in Tarrytown or made a run for it without them now. But what if the military really did hang her? He and Zack owed her something, maybe even their lives. Besides, even if she was helping the South, she had told them she did not carry secret messages, only notes to prisoners, and they were safe behind bars. When she was only a voice he had heard under the carriage in New York City everything was simpler.

He glanced at Zack who had closed his eyes. His father's words came to him as clearly as if he were in the room: "Son, God never meant for a man to own another human being as his slave." He looked at Zack, still sleeping, and swallowed hard. What if Zack had been born down South? The North had to win this war.

Zack opened his eyes wide and whispered, "You reckon it's time?" Slowly and quietly he sat up.

Just then Trim turned restlessly on his mat. Ben held his breath until the regular sounds of Trim's breathing began again. Motioning to Zack to follow, he stood, waited, then moved toward the door.

From his shirt front Zack took a piece of cloth and wrapped the door latch to muffle its sound. Together they slowly swung the door open. Ben held his breath as Trim muttered in his sleep then turned on his side away from the door. When they were in the dark, deserted hall Ben could hear his heart beating loudly. Zack touched his shoulder. His voice was so low, Ben barely made out the words. "Keep close to the wall till we come to the stair."

"Right," Ben whispered. Before them the hall looked like a dark, forbidding tunnel. Somewhere at its end were the stairs.

It seemed to Ben that every footstep might land him in a hole. The hall had looked long in candlelight, but in the dark it was as if it had grown even longer. At last the wall turned sharply. Ahead of them he saw the great staircase dappled in moonlight filtering through the leaded windows above the first landing. They stood for a moment, listening. The stillness of the night carried no sounds. With a sigh Ben moved reluctantly toward the stairs.

Somehow they were at the first landing, then climbing the second. The light from the first landing windows no longer reached them in the upper hall. Breathing hard, Ben gripped Zack's shoulder. "Zack, how are we going to find her room?"

Zack whispered back, "Counted six doors from the stairs carryin' that supper tray up here. We got to go by feelin' the wall and countin' doors."

Together they inched close to the wall, hands shoulder high, as they felt their way across the smooth wood paneling. "Door number one," Ben whispered. They passed it safely. At the sixth door, Ben whispered, "This must be it."

From his shirt he took the piece of white paper and slowly slid it under the black door. He could feel Zack's warm breath beside him. Almost without a sound the door opened partway, and he and Zack were pulled firmly inside. In the bright moonlight Ben saw before him the caped young man who had captured them. The young man smiled, and the illusion passed. The soft lines of Miss Jorgin's face became once and for all, for Ben, those of a beautiful young woman.

"The only way out that I know, besides the front door," said Ben, "is through the kitchen into the courtyard, unless we can open one of the kitchen windows at the side of the house."

Miss Jorgin nodded. "We'll try the window and stay close in the shadows of the house till we reach the woods. It must be well past midnight and time to go." Pulling her cape close, she said, "Everything depends on our reaching the river. But then, this isn't the first time you two have been on the river at night." Ben couldn't help grinning. Zack was silent.

Nothing stirred in the hallway as they made their way and strained to listen. Ben heard only the loud beating of his heart. Safely down the great stair they inched their way along with Zack leading, Miss Jorgin next, and Ben following. The way to the kitchen was shorter than the way he and Zack had come from Trim's room. In the moonlight the enormous iron pots looked like ugly monsters' heads squatting on their shelves. The huge fireplace leered like a hungry open mouth. Ben shook off his thoughts. They were close to the kitchen door when the sound of someone coming from the courtyard made Ben freeze. Quickly Zack pulled Ben by the arm while his other hand pushed Miss Jorgin ahead of them into the huge pantry behind the fireplace.

They flattened themselves against the wall in the shadow of the large hanging bundles of drying onions and herbs. Storage baskets were everywhere.

Sing kept his pantry full, though Ben had heard him say that he "had nothing to cook with." In front of him, directly at his feet, Ben made out the round shape of the cellar door's iron ring. Carefully he lifted the heavy ring and pulled. Miss Jorgin and Zack were on their knees instantly to help him. Together they lifted the trapdoor. Ben held it while Zack and Miss Jorgin climbed inside. Zack reached back to help as Ben slid his feet inside onto the rungs of the ladder. Gently they lowered the door into place. The blackness was complete.

Ben thought he had never seen such dark, if he could call it *seeing* dark. He tried not to think, just to listen. The footsteps had either gone or stopped somewhere above them. Ben couldn't tell. They waited; nothing but the sound of their breathing came. Ben moved as if to lift the trapdoor again, but Miss Jorgin, feeling him move, whispered, "Wait." They waited again for what seemed like a long time.

Miss Jorgin whispered again. "I've a candle." In another moment the small light of the candle flickered against the earthen walls of the cellar. Wooden stairs led down to a hard dirt floor.

"Mr. Jackson mentioned a tunnel leading from the water to the house. It was built in the old days for smugglers. The General's men bring in supplies that way. If this is the wine cellar, that tunnel must be somewhere down here." Miss Jorgin spoke softly, holding her candle high. She moved down the stairs and toward the far end of the room below.

The right end of the room was closed off by heavy metal gates. Beyond the gates, cases and barrels stood stacked against the walls. The part of the room they were in held only empty cases and wooden boxes.

Suddenly Miss Jorgin said excitedly, "Look here! There, behind those boxes to your left." She held her light high to show a black cavelike opening. Without hesitating, Miss Jorgin entered. Ben and Zack followed.

The tunnel twisted and sloped slightly downward. "We must be getting farther away from the kitchen side of the house, anyway," Ben whispered.

"Seems like some kind of cave to me, but I reckon it come out somewhere away from the house, maybe down by the river," Zack said in a low voice.

Then the tunnel branched off in two directions, and Miss Jorgin stood, uncertain about which way to go. The light showed nothing but more tunnel in either direction.

"We could try the left one first, and if it doesn't work come back and take the other way," Ben offered.

Miss Jorgin looked grim. "We have no time to waste, but I suppose it's the only thing to do. We'll try the left one." They walked in silence until without warning the narrow tunnel made a turn.

There was no doubt in Ben's mind that they had discovered an old dungeon. Four cells with heavy wooden doors barred by great iron bolts lined the walls. Small, narrow window slits were cut into each door.

Zack fingered his granny's charm. "Ben, you reckon they keepin' anybody down here?"

Ben's voice came out in a squeak. "Reckon nobody uses dungeons anymore—except foreigners." Silently he prayed, "Please, Lord, help us to get out of here."

A loud groan unmistakably coming from one of the cells made Ben grab hold of Zack. Miss Jorgin almost dropped her candle as she clung to the boys.

"Who's there? Who are you?" Miss Jorgin cried shakily.

"Sir Edward Broderick. For pity's sake, help me," answered the voice. Her hand shaking violently, Miss Jorgin lifted the candle high and moved slowly toward the first cell.

Ben felt rooted to the damp dirt floor, but as the candlelight moved away, he came to life. Both boys ran to Miss Jorgin's side.

"In here," said the voice. "Who are you?" it demanded almost in the same breath.

"We are prisoners like yourself, sir," Miss Jorgin said.

"Thank God, thank God." The man's voice ended in a choking half sob. In the light of the candle a man's face pressed against the small window opening.

"Stand back, sir, and we'll have you out of there," Miss Jorgin commanded. The heavy outside bolt, though it could not be reached from the high window in the door, was easily moved by the three of them, thus freeing the door.

The prisoner stood weakly holding himself upright against the wall. Miss Jorgin gave the candle to Zack and took a small bottle from her pocket. "This will help some," she said, holding it out.

"Thank you, sir, thank you." The man drank eagerly then handed the bottle back. "Where have you come from, and how in heaven's name did you get in here?" he asked.

"I am a Southerner, sir. My name isn't important. We must leave here without delay. I take it you are English, sir?"

"Sir Edward Broderick, owner of the *Nancy B.*, robbed of our cargo and sunk off the Canadian coast by these double-dealing thieves. We thought they were Confederate blockade runners, and as you know, our English sympathies are with the South. While I visited with their captain, their men boarded our ship. When the fighting broke out it was too late. In the confusion I managed to stow away. When they found me I was kept a prisoner. Eventually I landed here."

"And what of the stolen goods, sir?" Miss Jorgin asked.

"They are sold to the highest bidder in Nassau. The gang also sends small loads from Canada by way of the canal system and the river down through New York's ports. All of it is stolen, then resold for profit."

"Have you any word of the *Annabelle?*" Miss Jorgin asked.

"I fear she met the same fate as my own ship. While I was a stowaway, I saw the name *Annabelle* on an empty crate in the hold."

Miss Jorgin's face was white, and her hand trembled. "She was a southern blockade runner carrying cotton."

"I am truly, sorry, sir, for your loss," Sir Broderick said.

Zack sucked his breath in deeply. His eyes were wide. Ben felt himself shivering with sudden cold at the thought of the sunken ships. The men in the house were not loyal to any side. They were thieves and worse.

Miss Jorgin broke the silence. "There's no time to lose. We must find a way out of here. Can you tell us how they brought you here, sir?"

Sir Edward shook his head slowly. "I was brought in half-conscious through some sort of tunnel. The next thing I remember is waking up here in this cell."

Miss Jorgin had been busy lighting candles from her case. "Here, Ben, you and Zack take these, and you, sir," she said handing each a candle. "We must look over every inch of this place. There has to be a way out."

Ben and Zack took their lighted candles and walked carefully to the second cell. At its small window Ben held his light high.

The light quivered in his hand as he peered inside expecting to find another inmate or the bones of some forgotten prisoner. The cell was empty as were the next two. The room seemed to end at the far side in solid, damp, cobweb-hung earth.

"Over here, there's an opening," Miss Jorgin called to the others. Behind a large cask was a cave-like tunnel. Partway down, it branched off on either side. A short excursion through each showed a third and a fourth branching. All were dark, their packed earth walls damp and cold. All seemed equally hopeless. Silently Ben prayed for help. "Please, Lord, help us know which way we should go."

Zack constantly held one hand to his charm now. "Ben, all look the same to me, like somebody tryin' to fool whoever lookin' for a way out. You figure one of these the right way?"

Ben frowned. "Maybe we have to go back to where we started first. Remember, the tunnel forked there too." They were running out of time. Any minute their captors might discover they were gone and come looking for them.

Sir Edward came back from the tunnel he had been exploring. His face was pale, though his voice sounded better. "It looks to me as if the tunnel keeps going. It's a guess, but there isn't time to explore them all. I suggest we take it."

Miss Jorgin said simply, "Lead on quickly, sir." Ben and Zack followed. They moved at a fast walk into the inky blackness ever ahead of them. At first the sound of their own hurrying feet was all that Ben heard, but suddenly there was something else.

10

Terror

Zack heard the noise at the same time and reached out to grab Ben's arm. Something was coming, moaning and muttering as it came; its steps were heavy. The hair on Ben's neck tingled, and a chill raced down his spine. The terrible sounds were coming closer, as if the prisoners had awakened some evil thing living underground. Its shadow on the tunnel wall loomed huge and black.

"Back, back," Sir Edward commanded urgently. All of them flattened themselves against the wall. Zack's teeth were chattering, and Ben's heart seemed to stop as his throat tightened until it hurt. Sir Edward picked up a loose rock and raised it threateningly.

"Stop, I say, stop where you are," Sir Edward commanded. The thing stopped in the shadows just beyond the edge of the candlelight. Sputtering incoherently, it slowly began to come toward them.

"Trim!" Ben and Zack stared unbelievingly. "It's Trim, sir," said Ben.

"He ain't right," Zack added, "but he don't mean no harm."

Trim's stumbling gait and large frame had cast

huge, grotesque shadows on the tunnel walls. His heavy breathing and the noises he made had given the monsterlike effect.

Miss Jorgin approached Trim and gently laid her hand on his arm. "How did you find us, Trim?" she asked. Trim tried to speak, but the effort was too great. "You knew about the tunnel," she said, patting his arm. Trim nodded. "Is there anyone else following us, Trim?" He quickly shook his head left to right.

"Good. Good, Trim. Do you want to come with us? We have to hurry. The men you stay with are bad. Do you understand, Trim?"

Trim looked blankly at her. Miss Jorgin took his hand and pulled gently. "Trim, we have to go now, or the General and his men will hurt us if they find us. Will you come with us, Trim?"

Miss Jorgin tugged at Trim to pull him along the tunnel.

Trim shook his head no.

"We can't let him go back." Miss Jorgin's voice was despairing. "He could lead them to us."

Ben spoke up. "But he can't talk, ma'am, and he sure doesn't want to go with us."

At this, Trim took Miss Jorgin's hand and pulled back toward the way he had come. "No, Trim," she said, trying to hold her ground against his strong pulling. "Bad men, Trim. They will hurt us."

Zack stepped up to Trim. His voice was gentle. "Easy now, Trim. You tryin' to tell us somethin'?"

Trim nodded his head up and down forcefully.

Zack continued softly, "Good, good, Trim. You want us to go back to the house?"

Trim vigorously shook his head no.

"Trim, you tellin' me you want to take us somewhere? You gonna help us out of here?"

Trim's head went up and down affirmatively.

Zack patted Trim's arm and turned to the rest. "I think he knows the way out of here, and this ain't it."

Trim had let go of Miss Jorgin's arm. She picked up his large rough hand and patted it. "Trim, I'm trusting you." Holding Miss Jorgin's hand, Trim turned and began to walk back the way he had come. Halfheartedly, Ben followed with Zack and Broderick.

Sir Edward whispered to Ben, "Did you say 'ma'am'?"

"Yes," Ben whispered back. "She's a lady and an heiress too." Sir Edward said no more.

Ben jerked on Zack's shirt. "You think Trim knows what he's doing? Suppose he takes us all straight back to Sing's kitchen?"

Zack answered, "He ain't like other people, but he knows lots more than some folks. I trust him more than some folks too. Hey, Ben, you reckon they found our raft by now? Whole town's probably out lookin'."

Ben thought of his ma and pa. Maybe by now they had given up looking, thinking he had drowned. He could picture his pa praying, "Thy will be done, Lord." He was still alive, but if Trim had found them, would the General and his men be far behind? "What time I am afraid I will put my trust in thee," he whispered. A fresh rush of energy seemed to come from deep inside, and he hurried after the others.

Without stopping or hesitating, Trim led the group down a left branch of the tunnel as if he knew exactly what he was doing. It seemed like a long time had passed, but Ben had no way of knowing for sure. His candle still burned, and occasionally bits of the wax fell stinging hot on his hand.

"Hey," Zack pulled on Ben's arm, "you feel that?" From somewhere a breeze of cool air was rushing down the tunnel into their faces. Ben's candle flickered and nearly went out, but he cupped his hand around it and saved it in time.

Miss Jorgin's whisper came back. "The tunnel ends up ahead. Put your lights out and stay quiet." Before anyone could stop her, she had stepped to the tunnel exit, which was faintly lighted by the moonlight filtering through. She disappeared with Trim. Ben and Zack and Sir Edward came to the opening, which curved slightly upward and out into a thick clump of blueberry bushes. It was still night. The bright moon illuminated the dense surrounding woods and small outcrops of stone.

Ben whispered, "Zack, I can't see the house, but I don't see the river either."

Zack was puzzled. "One thing for sure, I don't aim on goin' back in no tunnel."

11

Escape to Canada

Miss Jorgin and Trim stood near the tunnel exit in a patch of woods. "It seems that Trim has found an old escape tunnel. We are north of the house toward the Catskill Mountains, but away from the river I fear." Miss Jorgin's voice sounded tired.

Sir Edward spoke up. "At least there are no guards here, and we've still time while it's dark to travel. We must get as far away as we can and find help."

Miss Jorgin looked at Trim. "The tunnel the men use to bring supplies from the river to the house, Trim, do you know where that tunnel is?"

Trim nodded his head up and down.

"Then why didn't you take us there, Trim? We want to go to the river," she said. Trim did not answer, and she tried once more. "Trim, there is a small boat near the river's edge. We need to use that boat to get away quickly."

This time Trim shook his head no.

Tired and upset, Miss Jorgin shook Trim's arm. "We must go to the river. You need to take us there through the tunnel."

Still Trim shook his head violently.

Zack stepped close to Trim. In a soft voice he said to Trim, "You tellin' us you know somethin' like it ain't safe for us to go back to the river?" Trim nodded his head up and down.

"Maybe the General's men be guardin' the tunnel by the river?" Forcefully Trim nodded his head up and down in answer.

"Are you sure, Trim?" Miss Jorgin asked. Again Trim nodded yes. "I don't know how you know, but I believe you," she said.

Something inside Ben flashed like a warning signal. He had imagined a quick escape on the river back to Tarrytown.

Sir Edward stepped between Ben and Miss Jorgin. "Forgive me, miss, but we ought to stay away from the river."

"So, you know who I am then," said Miss Jorgin.

"Yes, I overheard the boy mention it. You have nothing to fear from me. But I urge you to move quickly while we still have the advantage of a head start."

Miss Jorgin nodded her head in agreement. Turning to Trim she took his hand. "Will you go with us, Trim? I can't promise anything, but we will all do our best to escape to safety."

Trim shook his head slowly from side to side, then looked pleadingly at Zack. With one hand he made a small fist, held it close to him, and stroked it awkwardly with the other.

Zack watched him for a second. "He can't go. He

won't leave his rabbits or his bird," Zack said. Trim nodded yes.

"Poor lad," Sir Edward said. He picked up a rough branch for a walking stick and pointed it to the sky. Above them the stars were brilliant. "That way is north," he announced. "We may come upon a house, or a village, or at least a cave to shelter in."

No one except Zack noticed Trim steal away back to the tunnel.

There was no pathway to follow, and the going was rough. Wild bramble bushes scratched at Ben's arms and legs. Thorns caught at his clothes. Zack, now beside him, now behind him, was having the same trouble. Ben thought they had left the worst of the briar patch behind, when Zack stumbled into a thornbush. Ben waited while he struggled to undo the rag charm from the bush.

"Thing ain't worth a copper," Ben said impatiently.

"Don't you talk that way about Granny's charm, Ben. How you think we got safe out of that place?"

Angrily Ben yanked a branch out of his way. "I don't know why you wear the thing." He stomped ahead of Zack. His body ached with tiredness, and his stomach rumbled emptily. "Dumb, dumb. Never should have gone down to see the *Eagle*. Wouldn't be here now," he muttered. He and Zack ought to have tried reaching the river. Maybe they could have gotten to the boat without being seen. At least they would be on their way home and not headed in the wrong direction.

On and on the four pushed their way through the

thick brush and trees. Overhead the stars moved toward dawn. Ben thought they had walked for hours, when Sir Edward finally called a halt. "There's a clearing up ahead and a house," he whispered. "Thank God, I believe we've come upon a farm."

"What will we do if they're unfriendly?" Miss Jorgin asked in a low voice. "We have no weapons except my own." She held up her small pistol in the moonlight."

"Well, miss, we aren't exactly coming calling at a decent hour," Sir Edward said and laughed. Ben would have laughed if the whole thing hadn't been like a bad dream.

"I'll go first. If all is well I'll be back for you. If not, skirt the farm and go on. Keep north. Hide yourselves by day and walk by night."

Miss Jorgin laid her hand on Sir Edward's arm. "God go with you, sir. I believe the railroad is our best gamble now. If we can reach it, there is hope of our getting to Canada. The South has friends there who will help us."

Sir Edward nodded. "I have heard of the famous American Mr. Vallandigham, the man President Lincoln arrested for his speeches against the war. Living in Montreal, Canada, is he not?"

"Yes, Mr. Vallandigham is the very man I hope to contact," Miss Jorgin said.

Ben looked at Zack. Even in the moonlight Zack's face was stony with anger. Ben too felt a nagging worry. Both Sir Edward and Miss Jorgin were for the South. Back home the name Vallandigham meant one thing: copperhead. Somehow they had to get away. But how?

Sir Edward took a small paper from his shirt. "There is one favor I must ask of you," he said. "If anything happens to me, I would consider it a great kindness if you would see that my wife gets word. The address is here." He handed the paper to Miss Jorgin.

Ben swallowed hard. Zack whispered, "Walkin' in like that he could get hisself shot." Ben had heard of it happening, especially among hill folks who were suspicious of strangers. He only hoped they would not set the dogs on them.

Miss Jorgin sat on the pine needles scattered thickly beneath the trees. Her pistol lay in her lap. Her shoulders drooped with tiredness. A dog began to bark, and immediately all three of them looked up. Ben expected to see the animal come tearing through the clearing. In the farmhouse a window opened. A voice called out, and Sir Edward answered. After a short while a door opened, and Sir Edward went inside.

The minutes passed slowly. Ben's heart beat loudly. What could be happening in there?

Half an hour later Ben was eating the best bowl of soup he had ever tasted. The farmer stood by his stout wife, who watched her guests with a motherly eye.

"Thee art surely hungry," the Quaker woman said. and smiled at Ben and Zack. After they had eaten, Sir Edward and Miss Jorgin engaged the farmer in bargaining for three horses.

"We must go on to the train at Kingston as quickly as possible. In a few hours our escape will be discovered, if it hasn't been already. I believe they will not be expecting us to head for the train."

The farmer and his wife could not be hurried. Together they sat down with their hands folded and proceeded to meditate.

"Way will open," said the farmer and sat quietly. For the next few minutes no one spoke. Finally, the man smiled and said, "Thee must ride in the wagon. Wife, thee needs goods from town, and thee has been wanting to visit friends. Does not thee feel it is a proper time to visit?"

"Husband, thee art right. And thee has need of a new harness. Thee may fetch thee one in Kingston." Their hostess left the room for a few minutes and returned with her arms full. "Thee must go with hats to shade thy heads," she declared. The two large Quaker hats were for Sir Edward and Miss Jorgin. The boys' caps, though old and well worn, fit Ben and Zack. "Now thee looks better," she said.

The woman had also brought a shirt to replace Zack's torn one. "Thee art dark," she said gently, "but we will pray God to cover thee from all eyes that would harm thee." Even with the hat Zack was still Zack, though he looked a lot better with his new shirt, Ben thought.

Dawn turned to early morning as the wagon

jogged along the rough road. Ben closed his eyes. His stomach was full and his weary body burrowed gladly into the covering of hay the farmer had spread beneath them. The wagon frame and canvas cover hid them from view.

"Guess we ran into the right folks," Ben said sleepily. "Back home folks shun Quakers, but I can't see why." His voice drifted off into thoughts. "Way will open."

The hot July sun beating on the wagon brought Ben sharply awake. He was sweating. Sir Edward was sitting up behind the driver. Miss Jorgin sat in the far corner of the front of the wagon. Her hands were clasped around her knees, and her head rested on her arms. Zack lay asleep next to Ben at the back of the wagon. Through a small opening in the canvas Ben caught a glimpse of the houses and yards as they passed. Here and there children played, and dogs ran barking. The wagon passed a general store, and Ben thought this town looked pretty much like home.

"We're almost there," Sir Edward said. "If all goes well with the train we shall be in Montreal in about nineteen hours." Miss Jorgin nodded and went back to her rest.

Ben shook Zack's shoulder. "Come on, Zack, we're almost there." Zack woke with a start. His eyes became wide and dark.

"Where we at, Ben?" Zack sat up and wiped drops of sweat from his forehead.

Ben kept his voice low. "We're coming to the

train station. From there it's to Montreal and Vallandigham's people."

Zack spat. "No-good copperhead."

Ben whispered urgently. "Whatever we do, we've got to get back home."

Zack whispered back angrily, "Soon's we land outer here we can find our own way back. Run the river by night, hole up by day."

Ben felt like shouting, but he whispered back, "You don't think they're gonna let us go? Soon as we can find a way we will. But we've got to play along for now, unless you want to spend the whole war in Canada."

Zack grumbled. "Didn't say that. Ought to have gone to the river back at the tunnel."

Ben nodded. "Maybe, but listen, Zack," he whispered. "If this fellow Vallandigham thinks we're on his side we may have a better chance to escape. If anybody asks, just say you are a peace democrat. That means you're against President Lincoln and want to see the war over. You are for making a deal with the South so she can keep her slaves." Zack's face was defiant. "You know, that's what this Vallandigham and his followers want," Ben whispered. "Just think how my pa prays in the pulpit every Sunday for the government and the Union and for peace. All we need to do is forget the first part and stick with the last about peace." Still Zack said nothing.

Ben whispered urgently, "Listen, Jake Sorley called Pa a copperhead lover, didn't he? Well, I'm gonna say that's what some folks call Pa. It's some true, so don't go spoiling it. We've got to get back, right?"

Zack glared stonily at the back of the wagon and said nothing.

12

The Promise

With the hat on, Miss Jorgin looked quite different. Her pistol was nowhere to be seen, and she no longer carried the black bag, for Sir Edward had it.

Sir Edward had pulled his hat down close to his eyes. Ben pulled his own cap down and wondered if it would make a difference in his appearance.

The train came at last, sounded its mighty whistle, and screeched on its great wheels to a stop at the station. A few passengers stood waiting to board. At the far end of the station a group of Quakers waited. Shielded until the last second by the Quakers, Ben and Zack followed Miss Jorgin and Sir Edward into the train.

Ben's heart beat loudly in his ears. What if the General's men were here looking for them? Nervously, he glanced about. As the train moved slowly away from the station then faster and faster, a weight slid from his chest. They were getting away.

The deafening noise of the train whistle and the mighty speed as they flew past the countryside were exciting. For a while he forgot about what lay ahead.

In spite of the endless sights mile after mile, Ben finally slept. When he awakened, Zack was already staring out of the window at the crowded Canadian city, Montreal. At the station Sir Broderick secured a coach to take them to an inn.

"We shall soon be meeting your famous Mr. Vallandigham," Miss Jorgin said. She looked directly at Ben, then at Zack. "And you will be glad to know that soon our so-called friends Mr. Jackson and the General will find their business no longer welcome here." Her face had a determined look.

"And when I have made my report to the proper British authorities, neither man will dare show his face. I shall see them both hanged," Sir Edward said grimly.

"Does that mean Zack and I can go home then? I mean if the General and Jackson can't hurt us anymore, we won't have to worry. I know my pa will send money for both our fares home," Ben said eagerly.

"I wish it were that simple," Sir Edward said and turned his face to the coach window.

Miss Jorgin leaned forward toward the boys. "Sir Broderick and I have a difficult problem. We will be working together. I must finish my business in New York." She wearily leaned back against the seat. "I fear we must keep you company until we reach Tarrytown. We shall still require a head start; after that you will be free."

Ben felt his heart sink. He looked at Zack but could tell nothing from his set lips. It was all happening again. They were as much prisoners now as they had been at the General's.

"And I should add," Sir Broderick said, "that until the General and his men and Mr. Jackson are apprehended, none of us will be entirely safe. Once they get wind that we are in Canada, travel by train or boat back to New York will be extremely dangerous."

Ben had no more time to think. They had arrived at the inn. The innkeeper's wife made Sir Broderick and Miss Jorgin, who was still dressed as a man, welcome. Though the woman spoke only French, Sir Edward answered her easily. Ben recognized the two French words he knew: *merci beaucoup.*

They were seated in a small room where a serving girl brought in hot beef and ale. Miss Jorgin wrote a note and gave it to the woman, who disappeared with it.

After they had eaten, Ben and Zack followed Sir Edward out back to the privy. When they returned, Miss Jorgin was gone. The serving girl handed a note to Sir Edward, curtsied, then left.

"You may as well be seated, boys. It will be a short while before Mr. Vallandigham returns. Suppose you tell me how you came to be with Miss Jorgin." Sir Edward settled himself on a bench against the wall to listen.

Ben told the story, beginning with the coming of the mob from New York to Tarrytown. "You could call me and Zack peace democrats," he added. His tongue hardly paused over the small lie, though in his heart it felt large and heavy. "I guess you know

New Yorkers don't agree on the war," he said. "Some say the South is right, and we should stop the fighting; others say the war must go on." At least that was true.

Sir Edward nodded. "I've read your newspapers."

Zack had been fidgeting while Ben talked, and now he got up and went to the window. Ben heard him mumble something about copperhead. Sir Edward had leaned his head back and closed his eyes as though he had not heard Zack.

Ben stood and walked over to the window. Close to Zack's ear he whispered, "You've got to go along." Zack shrugged his shoulders and moved away.

Just then the door opened. Miss Jorgin entered with a gentleman: Vallandigham, the copperhead whom President Lincoln had banished from the North! Ben remembered seeing his picture in the newspaper. He swallowed hard.

Something like energy flowed from the man. Sir Edward jumped to his feet and bowed. "An honor, Mr. Vallandigham, to meet you."

Vallandigham bowed and held out his hand. "Sir Broderick, it is we who are honored by an Englishman such as yourself. My sympathy to you, sir, on the loss of your ship. We thank God for such men as yourself, and for England. I believe you and I must have a word with some important people who should be able to put a stop to the infamous Mr. Jackson and the General's trade here in Canada."

He paused and glanced at Ben and Zack. "Ah, our

two unfortunates. Miss Jorgin assures me you are peace democrats. Since she is willing to take the risk, I see no reason why you should remain here." He smiled, took leave of Miss Jorgin, and left the room with Sir Edward.

Ben stood with his mouth open. Zack stared silently as the men left.

Miss Jorgin laughed. "You must remember, these days even whispers carry far." Shame burned Ben's cheeks. She had heard everything! But if she knew, why had she not told Vallandigham the truth?

As if she had read his mind Miss Jorgin answered lightly. "One good turn deserves another. You were willing to help me leave the General's. If I can, I shall help you to get home. By tomorrow noon we will be on our way to Lake Champlain. The General will not expect us to take his very own route back. We will go by steamer bound for New York City. The boat will stop in Tarrytown."

Ben and Zack were both staring at her now. "But suppose we tell on you?" Ben blurted out.

Miss Jorgin answered slowly. "If you do, then I shall be sent to prison or perhaps hanged." The room was still as death, but her voice remained calm. "There is something I must try to get from the house where we first ran into each other."

"The Bleeker place, you mean," Ben said.

"Yes," she replied. "After that I will follow Sir Broderick on to New York City."

"Why are you telling us, if you mean to let us go free in Tarrytown?" Ben demanded.

"Once we reach Tarrytown all I ask is a head start to New York City—two hours—and then you are free to tell anyone you wish about us. Is it too much to ask? You must both give me your word of honor."

Ben swallowed hard. In war, one reported spies. To help the enemy was treason. But then, she was committing a kind of treason to the South by helping them get home! That she was a woman also bothered Ben.

Zack's face was set in determination, but he said nothing.

Miss Jorgin's low voice broke into Ben's thoughts. "I don't expect an answer now. Either I have your word, and you come with us to New York, or you may stay behind, here in Canada. I don't know for how long. Meanwhile, your room is upstairs next to mine."

At the door of their room she turned to look at the boys once more. Her eyes were deep blue, neither hard nor soft. "Remember that Mr. Jackson will have his men looking for his prize prisoners and for you, if for no other reason than for what you know. If you should try to leave without disguises and help, you could end up back in the kitchen with Sing. Then again, the General does not seem like a man of mercy. I fear your fate would be even worse this time." She left the room and shut the door behind her. A click from the outside told the boys she had also locked their door and taken the key.

Seated on the bed, Zack said, "Trouble sure followin' us."

Ben already knew in his heart that he did not want to betray Miss Jorgin, spy or not. But he couldn't blame Zack if he did. He sat silently on the single chair in the room and thought. Finally, he said, "Guess she did save our skins back at Old Man Bleeker's place, and she could have left us behind at the General's, but she didn't. On the other hand, she could just leave us here in Canada." He stood up and walked to the small window. "I'm not saying it's okay, but I'm thinking how the South can't get food in or cotton out. It seems a hard thing. Her trying to buy medicines and supplies is against the law, but the war is almost over, Zack, and we are winning."

"Well, we ain't won yet. Ben, don't you forget she ain't just a woman, she's a Confederate spy. She already tole you how she be carryin' secret messages to prisoners. Probably owns slaves too." Zack's face was hard with anger. He sat rigidly on the bed. "We can't let her go, Ben. It ain't right."

Ben glared at Zack. He knew it wasn't right, but she had not left them behind, and now she was ready to trust them with her life. "Anyway, what else can we do?" he asked. "You want to stay in Canada? Maybe Vallandigham will send us both to work on some copperhead's farm."

Zack swung his legs over the side of the bed. "Listen, Ben, I agree we got to go along with them now. But I ain't makin' no promise."

Ben turned his head away and thought fast. Even if he promised Miss Jorgin, Zack would not promise. And if Zack did promise, he would cross his fingers and break his promise as soon as he got the chance. Slowly an idea formed in Ben's mind.

"Zack, are you missing something?"

Zack stood up. "What you talkin' about?"

Ben's fingers closed tightly over the bit of rag and string stuck deep beneath the small stones and sling he carried in his britches pocket.

Zack's hand went to his throat; with a cry he was on top of Ben instantly. Over and over they rolled, knocking into the washstand, the bed, and now the wall.

Finally, Ben was able to pull free enough to yell. "Wait a minute, Zack. It's safe, and you can get it back. Besides, I didn't take it off you. It came off back in the wagon while you were sleeping. You might say I saved it for you."

Zack's fist poised in midair above Ben's nose. "How you mean, you saved it for me?"

Ben pushed Zack off his chest and sat up. "I'm telling you, it came off while you were asleep, and I just ain't thought much about it since. You can have it back."

Zack, as short of breath as Ben, sat where he was. "How come you didn't just give it back to me?"

Ben stuttered slightly. "I guess, I guess, well, you know. Pa says there ain't no such thing as a charm. A body just thinks there's something to it. Like wishing for a thing and making it come true by your own sweat. Anyway, here, take it. I wanted to make you promise you wouldn't tell on her until after." He held out the bit of rag to Zack. "Here. Take it."

Zack took the charm, inspected it, tied a fresh knot, and slipped it around his neck. He got up and straightened one pant leg. Ben stayed seated on the floor. Zack stared at him.

After a minute, Zack said, "You want me to promise her? I promise, hear?"

Ben looked up at Zack, not sure if Zack had crossed his fingers when he said it, but dared not to ask. "Thanks, Zack. I reckon it's our only way."

Early the following morning Miss Jorgin and Sir Edward arrived carrying several mysterious boxes. "I trust you have made up your minds," Miss Jorgin said calmly.

Ben looked at Zack, who nodded. "You have our word," Ben said.

"A head start is all I ask," Miss Jorgin said. "Good, now let's see how these do." She removed a dark wig from a box. Astonished, Ben watched her put on a short black beard. Next came the jacket and white collar of a minister, the kind some churches' ministers wore. On her head she placed a man's black hat. The finishing touch was a large cross on a chain around her neck. Ben gaped at the stranger who now stood before him.

"Now, Zack, you must dress like a schoolboy. You are under my care to be reunited with your mother, a former slave, who has been located in New York. Don't look so strange, boy."

Sullenly Zack took the clothes. On his neck Miss Jorgin hung a cross like her own. His hat matched hers too.

"Your turn," Sir Edward said to Ben, only it was a blonde-haired farmer who stood before Ben. He handed Ben a blonde wig. In a few minutes Ben looked as if he too had lived his life on a farm. The simple luggage he carried for his new farmer father completed the picture. He and Sir Edward would go first. They would take seats on the train as though they were traveling alone. Miss Jorgin and her pupil, Zack, would follow in another part of the train. The four would meet again at a certain inn.

The wig under the broad hat itched Ben's head, and sweat trickled down his neck. This was no plan of his. What if they did meet up with the General's men? He glanced at Zack, but the look in Zack's eyes only made him feel worse.

"Come, Nathan," Sir Edward said, "we must be off to the train." With a start Ben realized that he was Nathan.

13

A Dangerous Passage

By the time they arrived safely at the small-town inn, Ben's disguise no longer bothered him. He was beginning to feel like an actor, a daring one in his role as Nathan. Zack too looked his part. Whistling like the farm boy he might have been, Ben tossed his hat onto a chair.

"I'm afraid all of us must change our disguises," Miss Jorgin announced.

"Why can't we just stay like this?" Ben cried. A flash of indignation came over him. He had played his part well. "We've done okay so far," he stated. He watched warily as Sir Edward began to open the mysterious boxes again.

Miss Jorgin shook out the folds of what looked like a girl's dress. "On the train through Canada we were not so noticeable. The boat is a different story. You do not think we could arrive in Tarrytown like this?" Ben stared at her. He had not thought about it at all.

"Come now, Zack," Sir Edward said cheerfully, "let's see how white we can get you."

Zack backed away in protest. "Ain't no way you can make me white," he said firmly.

"You are right, Zack," Sir Edward said. "But we must try to disguise you the best we can. Our lives may depend on how well we do."

In the bustle of passengers the next morning, two Quaker women with their young daughters boarded the steamer *Le Luc*. The passengers went immediately to their cabin. It had been all that Sir Edward could do to get Zack into his dress with its long sleeves and high neck. A shawl, a large bonnet, high shoes, and gloves covered the rest of him. Most of all he had objected to the layers of stiff, paintlike makeup on his face, neck, and wrists. Even shadowed by the bonnet his face looked a sickly white framed by the long brown curls of his wig.

Ben fared little better than Zack. His dress was loose but hot. Under the bonnet his blonde wig made his head itch. The shoes felt awkward, the gloves tight and sticky. The final insult was a small drawstring purse dangling miserably from his gloved hand. All thoughts of daring had fled from his mind. What he wanted now was to hide somewhere.

Miss Jorgin had mysteriously added twenty pounds and ten years to her person. A severe Quaker bonnet hid most of her face. A pair of small, round, silver-rimmed spectacles set firmly on her nose. Though he knew better, Ben had the uncanny feeling that this woman and the real Miss Jorgin were truly not the same.

The change in Sir Edward was spectacular. His face, now clean shaven, also wore silver-rimmed spectacles. Beneath his large bonnet generous amounts of coarse gray hair showed. On his right cheek he had pasted two brown moles. Tiny dark age spots dotted the rest of his tanned face.

"I shall spread the word that Zack is recovering from a long bout with fever. That will explain why he is confined to the cabin," Miss Jorgin said.

Sir Edward said cheerfully, "I shall be right here with you, Zack. We will eat our meals in the cabin."

Zack did not answer. Ben thought he knew what was going on in Zack's head. At least they had been free to move around at the General's.

Miss Jorgin looked at Zack with a frown, then turned to Ben. "Remember, speak only when spoken to. Say thee, not you. We will make this as easy as possible. It should not be unusual if you also spend your time in the cabin with our invalid. But I'm afraid you and I must take our meals with the other passengers."

Ben could think of nothing to say. The thought of girl clothes and girl talk made him sweat in spite of the morning coolness. He would gladly stay inside the cabin. Without asking, he threw his bonnet off, removed the wig, and tossed them both onto one of the bunks.

Zack had already taken off his wig and hat. The heavy makeup made his unhappy face look like some tragic circus clown's. Ben tried not to meet Zack's angry eyes. He chose a top bunk and lay down fully dressed. Below him Zack gave a hard kick to the wooden bunk.

Sir Edward and Miss Jorgin sat talking in low

voices. The last thing Ben remembered was the slight soothing roll of the ship and their low voices trailing into his dreams. The steamboat's shrill whistle awakened Ben with a start.

In the tiny, sunlit cabin the wood paneling gleamed. Ben's eyes took in the built-in shelves, the curtained portholes. Once he had dreamed of a ship's cabin like this. Now he lay as if he were in that dream on a giant steamship speeding its way to the mighty river. Only this was real. Ben hung his head over the edge of his bunk and peered at Zack's painted face.

"You wantin' somethin'?" Zack grumbled.

"Nope, just wondering if you were awake."

Miss Jorgin was not in the cabin. Sir Edward, balancing a small mirror on his bunk, was carefully shaving away all traces of whiskers. He followed this with several applications of the light brown liquid that gave him his tanned look. Ben watched him paste on the two moles. His gray wig formed a large bun in the back. Sir Edward finished adjusting it and turned to the boys for inspection.

Ben whistled. "You really look like old Farmer Terhoeven's wife, don't he, Zack?"

Zack eyed Sir Edward, gave a half-swallowed grunt, and closed his eyes with an air of indifference.

A knock at the door brought both boys to a sitting position. Sir Edward was on his feet instantly. Holding his hand up in a signal for silence, he went to the cabin door and called through.

"Yes?"

Miss Jorgin's voice came back. "Wilt thee open the door, sister. I have a tray for thee and Sarah." In a minute the door was opened and a heavy, matronly woman entered. She carried a covered tray. Ben's heart seemed to beat faster whenever Miss Jorgin was near, but this person looked so little like her that he found himself thinking of her almost as a stranger.

"Come, Bertha. Thee art slow today and wilt make us tardy to the meal." The voice was Miss Jorgin's and Ben realized she was talking to him. A cold chill ran through him. Noon. He had forgotten.

In a few minutes, with his wig on and his bonnet straight, he stood by the door. His feet refused to move. With a desperate look on his face, Ben turned to Zack. He was grinning a wide, delighted grin. Ben's face flushed angrily, and then he was outside the cabin door following Miss Jorgin.

In the large dining salon Ben sat by a freckle-faced girl about his own age. She had a way of tossing her long blonde curls with a shake of her head whenever the talk turned her way. Her voice seemed never to come down from its high-pitched shrillness. With a boy's instinct, Ben disliked her immediately.

The girl's mother looked like one of those stiff women with feathered hats perched on their heads who sometimes came to the parsonage for tea. They were the kind who made his mother nervous before they came and glad when they left. A French family who spoke almost no English sat across from Ben and Miss Jorgin.

Because they were dressed as Quakers, Ben and Miss Jorgin were not the center of attention. Ben knew that people looked on Quakers as being odd in their ways. They were not well thought of back home either. Some folks found them easy marks for teasing because of their nonviolent ways. He had heard of one Quaker man who refused to resist when some town ruffians stripped him naked. No red-blooded man would allow a thing like that without a fight! Things were not quite as bad for Quaker women. After a while Ben found himself almost enjoying his role. Nobody seemed to notice him so that he felt almost safe. Talk flowed around them, mostly about the war. Once someone asked Miss Jorgin a question. Ben heard her reply in a modest, quiet voice.

The blonde girl with the shrill voice said something in French to the dark-eyed girl across from her and Ben. The pretty French girl's eyes sparkled as she replied in rapid French. Her small hands gestured while she spoke. When she finished she flashed a smile that showed her even white teeth. She waited, and smiled again at Ben. "Ne c'est pas?"

Miss Shrill Voice tossed her head and laughed. "Oh, you don't speak French, I'm sure," she said to Ben.

Ben was indignant. How did she know whether or not he spoke French? He didn't, but he wished now that he could. The French girl reached across the table and patted Ben's hand, which was resting flat near his plate. Ben blushed and quickly drew his hand back. For the rest of the meal he kept his eyes on his plate. When Miss Jorgin excused them, he nearly bolted in his eagerness to leave the salon.

On the passengers' deck a light breeze was blowing. The sun touched the ship's rails with brilliant dots of light. Ben stood at the railing with Miss Jorgin. Sailboats and small fishing boats dotted the lake. Folks waved as they passed. If he were captain of the steamer he would have ordered the wood poured on, the engine opened wide, "full steam ahead." The *Le Luc* would break all speed records. He was jolted back to reality by a tall figure in blue uniform.

"Afternoon, ladies." The soldier bowed his head slightly; his cap was in his hand. His eyes were dark under bushy black brows. For a second Ben thought of the General's eyes.

"You ladies traveling far?" Ben's heart beat fast, and the skin of his neck prickled.

Miss Jorgin smiled, then spoke. "The Quaker House in New York City be our destination. But first we must visit kinfolk near Tarrytown. Dost thee return from the war?"

"Oh, no," the soldier said and laughed. "My duty takes me this way. I'm a Vermonter myself. Have you been to New York before?"

"Yes. Hast thee heard of our society in New York? If thee hast time, I will gladly tell thee of its history."

"Well, I'd surely like that, ma'am," the soldier

answered. He cleared his throat and began to back away from the rail. "But I plumb forgot there is something I must be doing." He smiled apologetically and was soon out of sight. Miss Jorgin smiled at Ben, who grinned back weakly.

"Do you think he suspected something?" he asked in a low voice.

"Thee art skittish as a newborn colt," Miss Jorgin said lightly. "If anything, I wonder what brings a Union soldier, who is supposed to be on duty, here? One would think such a leisurely trip out of the question. I do not believe I have seen any other soldiers aboard."

Ben thought about it. She was right, and it puzzled him.

"Well, never thee mind. I am sure there is some good reason for his journey."

That evening, the ordeal of dining over, Ben and Miss Jorgin were heading back to their quarters. Twice he had almost forgotten to say thee instead of you and caught himself just in time. On deck the air felt cooler. A breeze had come up and turned the water choppy. The sound of a clink made him turn in time to see a bracelet roll past and flip over on its side. He stooped and picked it up.

"This yours?" he asked as he handed the bracelet back to its owner, the French girl.

"Merci beaucoup, mademoiselle," the girl said. She took the bracelet and curtsied.

"Ain't nothing," Ben answered. He looked away from the pretty young face smiling at him. With a sudden sinking in his chest his eyes met the dark eyes of the tall soldier who seemed to have come out of nowhere. Had the man heard his slip of the tongue?

Flustered, Ben made an awkward curtsy saying loudly, "Thee is welcome, miss," and hurried after Miss Jorgin.

All the following day Ben had an uneasy feeling whenever the Union soldier came in sight. What was he doing on the *Le Luc*?

Had he guessed about Ben? The man was friendly and asked politely after the health of the other young lady and her mother. Miss Jorgin's replies were always kindly. Still, he worried Ben.

They had just finished their noon meal and were on the way back when suddenly the soldier stepped from behind a pile of deck ropes. Ben felt his stomach sink. The man reached out to pat Ben on the head as he spoke to Miss Jorgin.

"Ma'am, I've been thinking it would be a pleasure to visit that Quaker House you mentioned. The one in New York City. I've never been to one of your meetings, but if time allows I sure would like to go once. Would you be so kind as to give me the address? If you put your name down, I'd like to remember who it was sent me there. Thank you kindly, ma'am."

Miss Jorgin reached into her pocketbook to remove a small writing kit. After a moment she handed a paper to the soldier. "Thee should'st follow thine own inner leading. If it brings thee to our meeting, thee wilt be welcome."

"Thank you, ma'am," the soldier said and stepped out of the way to let them pass. Ben felt a weight roll off him. The man was only curious about Quakers.

During the night the boat had stopped for engine repairs. When they finally reached the canal that would put it in the Hudson River, Ben had to report to Zack all that went on. Traffic was heavy, and boats of all sizes waited their turn to pass into the canal. Zack, restless and tired of being confined to the cabin, listened, asked questions, and sent Ben back to the deck to peer over the rail again and again for answers.

So far they had seen no sign of Mr. Jackson or the General and his men. If all went well they would be on the river soon. The closer they came to Tarrytown, the more anxious Ben grew. Sitting on the cabin floor he spun a marble he had found deep in his pants pocket. Zack spun it back to him.

"You ready, Zack? Tomorrow we'll be there." His eyes glanced at Miss Jorgin and Sir Edward, who were busy with some kind of map. In a whisper he added, "One thing's sure. I'll be glad to get rid of this dress."

Zack fidgeted with his rag charm, then spun the marble once more and leaned his head close to Ben's. "Now you thinkin' like I am. Soon as we dock, we home free."

Quick as a hawk Ben's hand closed on Zack's wrist. "You promised, remember?"

"I remember fine," Zack said in an angry whisper. "A head start, she say. Nothin' more, and that's all we be needin' to give."

Ben looked at Miss Jorgin, who was still busy tracing something on a map. He looked back at Zack. The look he saw in Zack's eyes made him silently mouth, "Fine. A head start."

14

Zack Disappears

Ben willed himself to ignore the itch at the back of his wig. Other passengers were finding their places for the evening meal as he and Miss Jorgin entered the salon. Nervously he slid into his seat. One more meal on board ship and this ordeal would be over! When Miss Shrill Voice and her mother did not appear, Ben felt relieved. He smiled at the French girl. He was safe, since she only spoke French.

The soft summer evening, cooled by a breeze rippling over the waters, brought many of the passengers to stroll the deck. Miss Jorgin too had decided to linger a while before returning to the cabin. Suddenly Sir Edward's fat Quaker figure hurried toward them.

"Thee sent for me from the ship's dining room, but I did not find thee there. Hast thee a problem?" he asked in a worried voice.

"Who told thee I sent for thee?" Miss Jorgin demanded quickly.

"I have a note from thee signed in thine own handwriting. 'Twas given me by the cabin boy." Sir Edward held up a bit of paper.

Miss Jorgin glanced at it. She quickly took hold

of Sir Edward's arm and hurried him back toward the cabin. Ben followed swiftly.

When Miss Jorgin knocked, the door opened to her touch. The cabin was empty!

Inside, with the door locked, the three of them stood mystified. Zack was gone. His wig lay on the floor. Someone had written a note to Sir Edward in Miss Jorgin's handwriting, but who?

Sir Edward looked grim. "The writing looked like yours. I thought I recognized it from the notes you showed me on the maps. Zack was here with me when the cabin boy came, so it wasn't Zack. Who else on board knows your writing?"

"No one knows my handwriting. How could anyone have written that note?"

Something made Ben think of the Union soldier. "The soldier," he wailed. "You gave him the Quaker House address and wrote your name too. He's on to us. I knew it."

"How could you know it?" Miss Jorgin demanded looking sharply at Ben. Ben stammered out the incident of the dropped bracelet. He could have bitten his tongue, his shame was so great.

Miss Jorgin began pacing the room. "You could be right," she said. "He is the only suspect we have at the moment. The question is, what to do next. He hasn't sounded any alarm if he does know something, or the captain would have sent for us. Whatever he is up to, we must find out. And where is Zack?"

Fear nagged at Ben. Could Zack have decided to leave on his own? Maybe he had jumped overboard hoping to swim across the river and get home somehow. If he had he could be somewhere in the area of the General's place right now.

A thorough search of the boat and the river showed no sign of Zack. "We must get into that soldier's cabin somehow," Sir Edward said.

"Perhaps two can play at the same game," Miss Jorgin replied.

A few minutes later, Sir Edward in his bonnet and shawl placed an empty tray in the ship's galley. "Thee art to be commended," he said pleasantly to the ship's cook. As Sir Edward lingered, the cabin boy appeared. Sir Edward reached out a closed hand and lightly touched the boy's coat sleeve at the shoulder seam.

"Boy, thee ought not let thy coat go so, or thee wilt fall apart in front of thy captain." A long rent in the material had appeared under Sir Edward's hand. "Thee art a good lad. I will mend thy coat and thee shall have it good as new for serving in the morning."

The boy looked puzzled and craned his neck to see his ripped coat. "Now ain't that something! Never even felt it or saw it at all. Ma'am, I'd be most obliged to you if you could fix it. It's a bad thing to happen to a new coat." The boy let Sir Edward help him remove the coat.

"Thee shall not worry thy head at all. Thee wilt find it here good as new in the morning." Sir Edward left quickly with the jacket.

It was still early evening. Many of the passengers were on deck enjoying the cool breezes. Ben felt almost odd in his boy's clothes once more. The cabin boy's jacket, mended rapidly by Miss Jorgin, was not an exact fit, but it would do if he didn't run into the cabin boy. He walked close to Sir Edward's swinging skirts and kept his head down. Miss Jorgin had found out the soldier's cabin number—C3.

The lower cabin area was empty. At the foot of the stairs Sir Edward slipped down the hall and flattened himself against the wall just beyond the door to cabin C3.

Ben's legs felt weak. Would the man recognize him without the wig and dressed as he was? Miss Jorgin had freckled his face heavily. He had to do this thing for Zack's sake. Suppose the soldier had kidnapped Zack? In his heart he heard the words "What time I am afraid I will put my trust in thee," and knocked at the cabin door.

A gruff voice called, "Who's there?"

"Cabin boy, sir. I have a message for you." The door opened slightly, and Ben looked up at the tall soldier and smiled. "Sir, the captain requests your presence right away, sir."

The soldier peered in the half-light at Ben. "Where's the other cabin boy? You ain't him."

Ben turned to run back toward the stairs as the man's huge hand reached for him. Without a word, the soldier's body fell against him. Quickly Sir Edward put a firm arm around the man and held him up as Ben placed one of the soldier's arms around his neck.

"Thee ought not to stay in the sun so long when

thy wound is only one month healed, nor drink so much," Sir Edward said in a motherly voice. Together they supported the unconscious man till they had him back in his cabin. "Thee wilt feel better soon," Sir Edward said as he shut the cabin door.

As they lowered the soldier to the floor he said, "I'm afraid I hit him rather hard. He'll be out for a while, I should think." Straightening up he drew in his breath sharply.

For a moment Ben stood still, not believing what he saw. Then he began to tremble violently. Zack, his bare back bleeding, leaned against the end of the bunk, his hands and feet tied, his mouth gagged. The layers of white makeup smudged in streaks on his face. His eyes looking at Ben were filled with hurt and anger.

Gently Sir Edward loosed his hands and feet and removed the gag. He held Zack against his chest for a moment.

"You okay, Zack?" Ben asked in a choked voice. "What's he done to you?" Anger flushed Ben's cheeks. He kicked hard at the soldier still slumped on the floor. He would have kicked again if Sir Edward had not stopped him.

"Son, that won't help," Sir Edward said. He laid a hand on Ben's shoulder. "Our job is to see that he's tied securely and gagged before he wakes up." Turning back to Zack he asked gently, "What happened, son?"

"He came in right after you left. I guess I didn't have time to put my wig back on. Next thing I know, he's makin' me put on the hat. Then he be sayin' how I better come quiet with him if I want to keep on livin'. Wasn't anythin' to do but go 'long," Zack said. "When we come in here, he tole me I was a no-count nigger, free or not, he don't care. He said he figure somethin' funny about you too, Ben, and how you sound like a boy. He said I better tell how come we be travelin' like that. Couldn't think of no thing good enough to tell him." Zack wiped his eyes.

When Sir Edward finished, it looked as if a soldier (minus his uniform) lay sleeping on his stomach. His face was turned to the wall, and a pillow was placed over his head to keep out noises. Sir Edward quickly searched the soldier's pockets. With a look of triumph he held up a handful of documents.

"These explain what our friend was doing on board ship. The man is a bounty jumper. Probably on his way to New York City to join the navy or the army this time. He'll take the bounty the army pays for volunteering, disappear, and begin all over again somewhere else. Each of these identification papers bears a different name."

"I sure wish we could turn him in," Ben said.

"Right," Sir Edward agreed. "But we have our own difficulties at the moment. We shall have to be satisfied that at least we have these."

While Sir Edward talked with Zack, Ben rolled the soldier's uniform into a tight ball. Minutes later he opened the cabin door and slipped into the hall. Sir Edward followed slowly.

Outside the door, he called loudly, "God give thee a long good rest. 'Tis what thee needs most." Inside the cabin the bound and gagged soldier made no answer.

From under Sir Edward's wide skirts Zack stifled a nervous laugh. He remembered the soldier's face close to his, and the smell of liquor. Hot tears coursed down his face as he held tightly to Sir Edward's waist under the large skirt.

Later that night Ben busied himself in a corner of the cabin while Zack rested lying on his stomach. Soft cloth bandages covered with ointment had eased the stinging flesh wounds. Two of the long, ugly scratches formed the shape of an X.

Sir Edward and Miss Jorgin sat on a bunk deep in conversation. Their voices were low.

"Unh," Ben grunted as his right arm jerked. Quickly he pulled his sleeve down and fumbled with something for a moment. He walked slowly over to Zack's bunk and sat on the edge. Zack lay there lazily. Then suddenly his eyes grew wide. He grabbed Ben's arm. "You're bleedin'! What you done, Ben?"

"It's nothing, just slipped with my knife." Ben rolled his sleeve up past the elbow for Zack to see the two long scratches in the shape of an X.

"Smaller than mine," Zack said. "Guess that don't matter. You done it, and that's what counts."

Ben nodded. "Sort of like Indians do when they make blood brothers, I guess. Reckon I'll stick some ointment on it now."

15

The Return

The night passed slowly for Ben. What if the soldier worked his way free and came for them? How could he explain to the captain why he and Zack had not turned in Miss Jorgin and Sir Edward right at the beginning? He had made a promise to help her, but didn't it make him a traitor to his country? Zack too? Like a heavy weight the problem sat on his chest. In his heart he knew, traitor or not, he had wanted to make the promise and would keep it as long as he could.

If he had not crept out of the house that night to go rafting, none of this would have happened. "I confess it was wrong to do, Lord," he whispered. Maybe his mother and father figured he and Zack were drowned. His eyes filled with tears. "I never meant to hurt them, Lord," he said.

As if he were in church he could hear his father's voice calling sinners to repent. "I feel like I can't do right no matter which way I go, but I want to, Lord." His eyes were heavy with sleep. He awakened suddenly in the darkened cabin where moments before he had seemed to be somewhere else. He must have been dreaming. The regular breathing of the others still asleep was the only sound.

In his dream he had stood in a meadow in the fading light of evening watching a long line of sheep that stretched as far as he could see. In the dimness he saw the dark forms of large wolves snapping at the heels of the sheep as they walked. At the head of the line of sheep a great lamb, larger than any of the sheep, led the flock. One enormous wolf with bared fangs snarled menacingly at the lamb, but the great lamb showed no fear. Ben had awakened with tears trickling down his face. The dream stayed in his mind, somehow soothing away the nameless fears that had nagged him. He felt the gentle rocking of the ship, and soon drifted into an untroubled sleep. He awakened feeling as if he had just been held close in loving arms. A tear trickled down his face. Like the others in his dream, he had felt the threat of evil, but it was as though the Lord had led his sheep toward safety. Rolling over he drifted into a peaceful, dreamless sleep.

When morning came, the sun was bright. Ben felt a gladness in spite of the fact that they were still prisoners. In a short while they would be in Tarrytown.

Miss Jorgin looked grim as she faced Ben and Zack. "We can't leave you at the inn in Tarrytown as planned. It's only a matter of time now till that soldier awakes and somebody discovers him," she said. "We must be the first ones off the boat. In a few minutes we'll be docking. For all our sakes keep close to Sir Edward and say nothing. As soon as we are safely away to the Bleeker house we can all breathe easier."

Ben stared at her. This close to home, nothing else seemed to matter. "You can go on to Bleeker's if you want, but Zack and I are going home."

In a patient voice Sir Edward explained. "Our encounter with the soldier has changed things somewhat. We dare no longer take a room in the inn. Our plans were for you boys to stay in the inn long enough to give us a little time, a head start. Now you will have to come with us to Bleeker's. After that we shall leave you there, and you will be free to return."

Zack turned his head so that his Quaker bonnet completely hid his face.

"A promise is a promise," Miss Jorgin said softly. "Just a little longer is all we ask."

Unable to answer, Ben nodded his head. Sir Edward took both boys' hands in a firm, "motherly" grip.

Now the four were walking down the plank. Ben tried to keep his eyes turned away from familiar faces. At one point he saw the bent old figure of Zack's Uncle Uriah. Goose bumps rose on his neck. They were close enough to call out!

The group walked straight on away from the waterfront to the stable where Miss Jorgin arranged for a carriage. Within a few minutes they were on the way to Old Man Bleeker's place, every mile taking them further from home.

They were beyond the town into the shelter of

the woods lining the dirt road. Zack had removed his bonnet and wig. With the skirt of his dress he rubbed at the heavy makeup on his face.

"Here," Miss Jorgin said, handing him a handkerchief dabbed with ointment. "Rub this grease on and it will come off."

"Don't need no help," Zack muttered and continued to scrub at his skin.

"Suit yourself," Miss Jorgin replied.

Quickly Ben removed his own wig and bonnet. He slipped the girl's dress off over his head. The shoes would have to do, since he had left his moccasins behind. From the girl's purse he rescued his sling shot. The disguise lay in a rumpled heap at his feet. When his eyes met Zack's he saw relief in them.

The Bleeker place looked deserted enough. Sir Edward lost no time in breaking open a shuttered window. Once inside he disappeared and returned shortly dressed in his own clothes.

"I shall take one of the carriage horses," he stated. Miss Jorgin nodded. "God go with you till we meet," he said. Turning to Ben and Zack he smiled and winked. "You two shall make fine young men one of these days. I hope we may meet again under better circumstances." Before Ben or Zack could say anything he was gone.

Miss Jorgin had removed her own disguise. Once more Ben saw the young face of Miss Jorgin. Only this time she wore the uniform of a Union soldier! She smiled, and Ben's heart turned over.

"Now to take care of one small matter, and I too shall be off," she said. "You might like to see what the General has made of this place," she added.

Ben felt Zack nudge him. "You reckon the General's men be followin' us here?"

A shiver went down Ben's back. In this deserted place anything could happen. "I don't know, maybe," he said.

Holding a lighted candle, Miss Jorgin led the way into the cellar. Ben drew in a sharp breath. The place was piled with boxes and barrels.

"Some of this stuff is too dangerous for the General to take into New York City's port all at once. This is where he keeps it until it can be taken through safely." She scanned the boxes till she found what she wanted.

She opened one and rummaged through its contents. With tears in her eyes, she looked up. "Medicine," she whispered. "Quinine, morphine, things our hospitals need desperately in the South. I must take these," she said, then checked the contents of another similar box.

Ben helped, and Zack too, as she set aside all the boxes of medicine she could find. Together they lugged them upstairs and out to the waiting carriage.

When they had loaded them all she faced the boys with a solemn look. "I must be off," she stated. "Try to understand. The South is fighting for her own freedom, for her very life. If it were not for this war, we could have been friends." Tears flowed down her face. "I have brothers, no older than you."

She wiped her eyes with the back of one hand. "Now I have your word of honor. I shall believe it is enough."

Ben could not find words to say. Beside him Zack stirred. "I'll see to the horse," he said. Miss Jorgin nodded.

While he talked gently to the horse, Zack worked on the carriage harness so that Miss Jorgin could manage the single horse that must now do the work of two. When he was through he helped her up. She would have to manage carefully. "Reckon if you talk to him softlike he'll do okay," Zack said.

As Miss Jorgin rode off, slowly at first, then out of sight at a gallop, Ben said, "Never thought you'd take kindly to helping her."

"Reckon that makes us even," Zack said. "Now what we supposed to do?"

Sounds of a rider heading their way made Ben start. In a flash the two of them disappeared into the woods.

From behind a screen of thick bushes they saw the rider reign in his horse at the front of the Bleeker house. Even from this distance Ben recognized the man. It was Mr. Jackson.

They watched as he unlocked the front door and entered the house.

16

A Matter of Heart

We got to do somethin' now," Zack said. "Once he finds out somebody's been here he'll take off."

"What can we do?" Ben whispered.

"You stay here, Ben. We be needin' that horse."

Ben's heart thumped as Zack slipped from behind the bushes. Jackson could return at any second. If the horse neighed or bolted from Zack, then what? "What time I am afraid, I will trust in thee," he whispered.

Zack approached the horse and laid a hand on its neck. His head was close to its ear. Slowly he led it back toward Ben. Zack mounted, and Ben got up behind him. At first they quietly made their way through the trees until they were far enough from the house to take to the road.

"Hold on," Zack ordered and dug his heels into the horse's sides. "That' it. You doin' fine," he said as the horse began to run.

"We've got to tell the marshal about Jackson and the Bleeker place," Ben shouted. He clung to Zack as the horse galloped wildly.

"Right," Zack called back, continuing to keep the horse at a swift pace. Relief washed over Ben. They were getting away.

Folks on Broadway gaped as the boys raced by into town. At the marshal's office Zack pulled the horse to a stop. Inside, the marshal was about to drink from a cup of coffee.

"Well, I'll be," he uttered. A look of astonishment flitted across his face.

Without a pause, words poured from Ben. "We were kidnapped at Old Man Bleeker's place. There's a whole smuggling ring that's selling illegal goods to the South using Bleeker's place for storage. A man by the name of Mr. Jackson runs it. His man called the General has headquarters up the river between here and Kingston. You can't see it from the river." Ben took a breath and went on. "They're running boats up to Canada for supplies, then downriver to New York City. Some of the stuff stays at Bleeker's till it's safe to take it on. Marshal, you got to hurry. Jackson is alone out at Bleeker's right now. Don't know what he'll do once he finds his horse gone."

One of the marshal's men who had come into the room along with three others spoke out. "The boy's right about the horse. Seen a fellow riding that horse a while ago. It's the same one these two rode in like his tail was on fire."

The marshal looked hard at Ben. "Can you describe this Jackson?"

"He's tall as my pa," Ben replied. "Dark hair, thin

mustache, blue eyes, handsome, dressed like a gentleman, and he has a southern accent."

"I saw a fellow like that earlier over at the stables," one of the men said.

"I want you boys to stay right here until I get back," the marshal said. Ben's heart sank. "On second thought," the marshal added, "your folks will be mighty glad to see you. Both of you go on over to the parsonage. Your pa can send for Zack's granny. Just you be there when I get back. I'll be needing the whole story from you two." Reaching for his gun, the marshal rose. "You men come with me," he said. "Let's take a look at Bleeker's."

No one mentioned the horse. Gratefully, Ben and Zack mounted once more and rode to the parsonage.

In unbelief, pale as though she might faint, Ben's mother stood motionless at the kitchen door. She trembled as she sank to her knees and reached out her hands to touch Ben. Then she was holding him tightly and crying.

"Ben, oh, Ben, where have you been this long time? What happened to you?" Her free arm reached out to circle Zack.

Ben's father stood at the kitchen table. His lips moved silently, wordlessly, as if in prayer. Tears ran down his face. In one great stride he was by the boys, and his long arms enfolded them both.

"Son, it's the Lord's miracle. We thought you drowned, both of you. The Lord God be praised!" His voice choked. When he had again regained control he asked, "Well, son?" He stood looking down at Ben no longer only as Ben's father but also as judge and minister all at once.

Ben hardly knew how to begin. It all seemed so wild and unreal. A momentary picture of Miss Jorgin, pale and beautiful even in her soldier's uniform, passed through his mind. Every minute of delay added to her hope of escape.

"Son," his father said gently.

A wave of love mixed with sorrow nearly choked Ben. He was a traitor to his country, to the Union. He could barely bring himself to speak.

"Ben, you're not hurt, are you?" his mother asked anxiously.

"No, Ma, I'm fine."

"Yes, ma'am, we both jus' fine," Zack echoed.

Ben began to tell the story starting with his and Zack's rafting out to see the *Eagle*. How clearly the whole thing came back, as if he could never forget a single detail. "So the marshal and his men have gone for Jackson right now," Ben finished.

"And for Miss Jorgin and Sir Edward," his father added.

A lump filled Ben's throat. He looked at Zack, whose gaze was turned toward the floor.

"Not exactly, sir," Ben said lamely. "What I mean is, the marshal doesn't know yet about Miss Jorgin or Sir Edward."

"What do you mean he doesn't know yet?" Ben's father demanded.

"Means we didn't tell him," Zack said. "Didn't 'xactly have a chance the way the man ran out that office to catch that Jackson fellow. Didn't ask no questions. Didn't wait for no details."

"Look at me, Ben," his father commanded. Ben looked into his father's steel-blue eyes. For a minute neither spoke.

"I didn't tell him on purpose, Pa. Guess that makes me a traitor, don't it?"

With a groan Ben's father turned away.

"Oh, son," his mother said, "you ought to have told the marshal. By now Miss Jorgin and her friend have such a head start they may not be able to find them. Once they reach the city it might be impossible." She sighed deeply. "You don't know the ugly rumors that have gone about in town ever since the day the mob came for the draft lists. Some folks think your father was in sympathy with the mob and that's why they turned back. What will they say now, when they hear about this Miss Jorgin's escape?"

Ben's throat ached. He had forgotten Jake Sorley's taunts calling his pa a copperhead that day.

His father groaned and sat down at the table. "I taught you that a man must keep his word. But this is wartime. The marshal must be told, however late it is."

Silence filled the kitchen. Ben could feel it pressing in on him. Zack hung his head.

Ben's mother looked at him with pain in her eyes and around her mouth. Then suddenly her eyes flashed, her voice was sure and firm. "And did you not also teach them mercy, Stewart? Why else would she have taken the boys out of danger? She could have slipped away from that den of robbers without them. She could have left them in Canada. Tied them up on the boat and left them to the mercy of the captain or that horrible soldier, but she didn't. She wouldn't leave them behind! Oh, Stewart, we owe her a chance for her life. She risked her life for theirs."

The Reverend Stewart Able let his head sink forward into his hands. No one spoke.

The clock on the mantel filled the room with its ticking, ticking the precious minutes away. As he listened to the clock it seemed to Ben like the hoofbeats of two horses galloping further and further away toward escape.

At last his father looked up. He stood with his hand on his wife's shoulder. "My dear, your heart has a wisdom above this war and its demands. You would have been a second Rahab. You recall the Bible story, boys," he said. "Rahab, the Canaanite woman, hid two Israelite spies in her house and told the king's soldiers she had not seen them. The spies got away safely, and Rahab became a heroine for doing what she believed was right.

"I'm afraid you may not become known as heroes, but you have done what you thought in your hearts was right." He paced the floor in thought. "The marshal must know," he said. He stopped to look at the boys. "You have already managed to give Miss Jorgin a little time as you promised." He looked hard at Ben. "The marshal will be angry, rightly so, but

I do not think you have much to fear. The man himself did not ask you for more details. It was an omission on the marshal's part that he will not be soon willing to make widely known." The corners of his mouth turned up slightly. "The quality of mercy," he said as if to himself. Then he placed a hand on the boys' shoulders and said firmly, "As for being traitors, I believe that both of you boys are as loyal in your hearts as any man in this town."

"Thank you, Pa," Ben whispered.

Zack grinned. "I'm right glad too, sir."

Reverend Able smiled back at Zack. Suddenly with a great laugh he picked him up, swung him high into the air, and landed him back on his feet. Ben smiled at the old familiar joy of his father's ways. Then he noticed Zack's neck.

"Zack, it looks like you've lost Granny's charm again."

Zack's hand reached up out of habit to the empty place where the old rag had hung.

"Don't need it none now. I tole God if he got me out of that trouble with the soldier when things was lookin' real bad, I'd know he was the one who done it. And he sure done it."

"Didn't I tell you so?" Ben said. A great weight seemed to have rolled off his shoulders.

As his pa predicted, the marshal had been angry. He had not found Miss Jorgin or Sir Edward, but Mr. Jackson was in prison. The Bleeker place was shut down for good this time. The marshal had received a commendation. Ben smiled. Some folks even thought he and Zack were heroes. Of course, there were those like the Sorleys who would not forget that two others had escaped.

While the kidnapped Ben and Zack were moving far up the Hudson and into Canada and back, the North had fought and won the battle of Gettysburg. The North and the South each lost over twenty thousand men who were either killed or wounded in the battle. Maybe somehow Miss Jorgin did get her medicines through. Ben wondered for a long time.